Books We
er Books Weekly Reader Books Weekly
der Books Weekly Reader Books Weekly Rea
eader Books Weekly Reader Books Weekly R
y Reader Books Weekly Reader Books Weekly
ly Reader Books Weekly Reader Books Week
ekly Reader Books Weekly Reader Books We
eekly Reader Books Weekly Reader Books W
Weekly Reader Books Weekly Reader Books
s Weekly Reader Books Weekly Reader Boo
ks Weekly Reader Books Weekly Reader B
ooks Weekly Reader Books Weekly Reader
Books Weekly Reader Books Weekly Read
er Books Weekly Reader Books Weekly Re
ader Books Weekly Reader Books Weekly
eader Books Weekly Reader Books Week
y Reader Books Weekly Reader Books Wee
ly Reader Books Weekly Reader Books W
ekly Reader Books Weekly Reader Books
Reader Books Weekly Reader Books

FIRE STORM

A NOVEL BY ROBB WHITE

From the first ominous curl of smoke and tiny, crackling flame, the ranger saw the fire spread quickly along the high ridge where the power lines ran. Now, driven by a steady, hard wind, it was pouring down through the drought-plagued forest, creating its own furious hurricanes and spreading all across the foothills and into the canyons.

It was the work of an arsonist, the ranger knew, who must still be near by. In a gripping and suspenseful account, Robb White paints an unforgettable picture of a huge forest fire that not only devastates everything in its path, but traps the ranger and the young boy he is pursuing as well.

FIRE STORM

Weekly Reader Books presents

FIRE STORM

a novel by

Robb White

DOUBLEDAY & COMPANY, INC., GARDEN CITY, NEW YORK

This book is a presentation of Weekly Reader Books.
Weekly Reader Books offers book clubs for children
from preschool through high school. For further
information write to : **Weekly Reader Books,**
4343 Equity Drive, Columbus, Ohio 43228.

Edited for Weekly Reader Books and published by
arrangement with Doubleday & Company, Inc.

Library of Congress Cataloging in Publication Data

White, Robb, 1909–
Fire storm.

SUMMARY: A raging forest fire in the National Parks
area of the Sierras traps a forest ranger and a young
boy he suspects is an arsonist.
[1. Forest fires–Fiction] I. Title.
PZ7.W5844Fi [Fic]

Library of Congress Catalog Card Number 78–72186

ISBN: 0-385-14630-2 Trade
ISBN: 0-385-14631-0 Prebound

PRINTED IN THE UNITED STATES OF AMERICA

Also by Robb White

THE LONG WAY DOWN

DEATHWATCH

THE FROGMEN

CANDY

SILENT SHIP, SILENT SEA

SURRENDER

THE SURVIVOR

DEEP DANGER

FLIGHT DECK

THE HAUNTED HOUND

THE LION'S PAW

MIDSHIPMAN LEE

MIDSHIPMAN LEE OF THE NAVAL ACADEMY

THE NUB

SAIL AWAY

SAILOR IN THE SUN

SECRET SEA

THE SMUGGLER'S SLOOP

THREE AGAINST THE SEA

TORPEDO RUN

UP PERISCOPE

NO MAN'S LAND

OUR VIRGIN ISLAND

IN PRIVATEER'S BAY

RUN MASKED

Motion Pictures

HOMICIDAL

HOUSE ON HAUNTED HILL

MACABRE

13 GHOSTS

THE TINGLER

UP PERISCOPE

VIRGIN ISLAND

I have dedicated books to
aunts, wives, in-laws,
friends, and lovers; to one
dog and two myths; so this
book is for

ROBB WHITE III

FIRE STORM

-1-

The angry man on the horse suddenly realized that he had ridden too far into this valley.

He had been so intent on catching the arsonist who had set this fire, and so outraged, that he had forgotten his own safety and was now threatened from two directions.

This forest fire was very serious. Started by an arsonist on the high ridge where the power lines ran, it was pouring down through the drought-plagued forest. Driven by a steady, hard wind, the fire was also creating its own furious hurricanes, which kept spreading it all across the foothills and down the canyons. Smaller fires, set by blowing embers, were starting up everywhere.

The man on the horse hated to let the arsonist get away, and despised him, but now he had no choice but to turn and run for his life.

He was turning the horse, the reins pressing against the horse's neck, his body leaning into the turn, his knee pressing the horse to turn, when he heard a shrill and frightened screaming.

Hesitating, taking the turning pressure off the horse, the man listened and heard the sound again.

Some hiker, or camper, or hunter was also trapped by the fire and, from the sound of his voice, was already hysterical with fear.

The man on the horse turned toward the sound and drove the horse forward.

The scream now seemed to be a name, a long-drawn-out calling of the name "Annnn—neeee! Annnn—neeee!"

There must be two of them out here, the man on the horse thought, as he rode hard through the smoky air, trying to locate the screamer.

Through his own fear, the man on the horse had a small, clear thought. This horse was tired, the smoke was hurting his lungs, the fire was frightening him. The man hoped that whoever was screaming, and Annie, were small, perhaps even children, for the horse would have great difficulty carrying three heavy people the distance and at the speed necessary to get clear of the fire.

He was close now, the screaming nearby and loud.

And then, as the horse broke through a small thicket of dry brush, there was the arsonist.

There was no doubt in the man's mind about that. There was the same blazing, red, plastic-looking shirt that he had seen when the fire had first started. And strung over the man's shoulder was the same long-handled butterfly net the arsonist had been carrying.

But what really convinced the man on the horse was the fact that the arsonist, screaming hysterically, was not running away from the fire. Instead he was running straight toward it.

That's the way arsonists are, the man on the horse thought bitterly. Crazy. They *had* to be crazy to do the things they did.

That was no excuse for this murderous fire, and the man on the horse began to shake with rage as he rode toward the man running on the ground.

His hatred for this man became absolute as he caught up with him and leaped straight out of the saddle.

The man was still screaming "Annnn–neeee!" as the man from the horse grabbed him by the shoulders, stopped him in his tracks, and then spun him around. Holding the reins with one hand, he caught the man by the throat and shoved him out at arm's length, holding back his other hand in a fist, ready in case the man made a move.

Holding him that way, the man from the horse almost *wanted* the man to make some sort of move. For a knife, perhaps, or a gun, or even a hand. He'd better not move a muscle, the man decided, or I'll hurt him.

But the man did not move at all; just stood there, gasping for breath, as the fingers on his throat choked him.

And it wasn't even a man. Just a boy, maybe fourteen, fifteen. His face was filthy with sweat and ashes and now tears of pain.

But the boy's gray-blue eyes, tears making them glisten, looked directly at the man, the eyes not blinking, and showing no fear. And no craziness.

This steady, calm, and direct gaze bothered the man for a moment until he remembered how clever these crazy people could be. People who knew them, even their parents, never even suspected what terrible things they did when they sneaked off alone with their hidden matches, or fire bombs, or delayed-fuse igniters.

This thought brought the man's rage seething up again and he turned loose the boy's throat, grabbed him by the shoulders, and began to shake him so viciously that the boy's head snapped wildly around. But even in this wild movement of his head, the man saw the boy's eyes still looking at him, unblinking, calm, direct.

Gradually the man stopped shaking him and then, at last, let his hands drop. For a moment the boy and the man stood without moving, and in silence, as they looked at each other, the man's eyes hard and glazed with anger, the boy's calm and now strangely compassionate, as though he felt sorry for the man.

Then the boy slowly raised his hand and rubbed gently at where the fingers had bruised his throat.

The man stepped back one pace and leaned down a little to get closer to the boy's face. And then, his voice low and vicious, he said, "There shouldn't be any law to stop us from killing people like you right where they stand. Just killing you whenever we can."

"But there is a law, isn't there?" the boy asked.

"SHUT UP!" the man bellowed at him, shaking him again. "SHUT UP!" Then he turned him loose and stepped back. "You set this fire, didn't you? Up on the high ridge by the towers. You set it, didn't you?"

The boy seemed to hesitate a moment before he said, his voice vague, "The fire?"

"SHUT UP!" the man yelled. "And don't act crazy with me. You set it. I was there and I saw you." He reached out and grabbed the red shirt. "Same shirt." Then he grabbed the butterfly net and yanked it off the boy's shoulder. "And this ridiculous thing."

The man threw the net down on the ground and broke the handle with his foot. "And I saw you run. And this is the direction you ran in."

The man stepped back from the boy and said in a low, slow voice, "You little. . . ."

"You saw me run?" the boy asked quietly.

"SHUT UP!" the man yelled at him. Then, his voice suddenly quiet and menacing, he said, "If there's anything I really hate, it's an arsonist, a firebug. Oh, maybe murderers are worse, but then you're next. Setting fire to houses, burning up the people, even women and little babies. Setting fires to the forests and killing all the animals and trees, and every living thing."

"Wait a minute," the boy said, "I . . ."

The man grabbed him but didn't shake him, and his voice was still controlled as he said, "When I'm talking to you, you keep quiet. You understand? You don't talk when I'm talking."

"Yes, sir," the boy said.

"You're lucky," the man said. "I know guys on Tower Patrol who would kill you right here and let it look like the fire did it. I'd like to do it myself, but I'm not going to. You're under arrest."

"Why?" the boy asked quietly.

"*Why?*" the man yelled, then grew quiet again. "Because you're an arsonist. You set these hills on fire and it's going to burn for *miles*, killing everything, all the trees, even the little bugs. The land's going to look like a scar. So I'm arresting you because you set this fire—on purpose."

The boy's voice was very calm as he asked, "Did you see me do it?"

"I didn't have to see you set it. You were up there where it started, and there was nobody else. So it had to be you."

"Nobody?" the boy asked, his voice very low and almost breaking.

"That's right. Nobody else but you. So you set it, didn't you?"

The boy's voice sounded as though it was trembling a little, and was hardly more than a whisper. "Nobody—else?"

"Are you deaf and crazy too?" the man demanded. "There was nobody else. You set this fire all by yourself. You understand that?" Then he leaned close to the boy and said slowly, "You did, didn't you?"

"Am I supposed to answer that," the boy asked quietly, "or are you going to yell at me again?"

"Answer it, stupid!"

The boy's voice was quiet and no longer trembling as he said firmly, "Yes. But I—"

"That's all!" the man yelled at him. "That's all I want to know. I don't want any excuses, any lies. You can tell them to the jury but it isn't going to do you any good. They're going to *fry* you, kid."

Then the man stood up very straight and said as though he were reading something, "I hereby arrest you in the name of the law."

The boy just stood there looking at him with those calm, blue eyes. At last he asked quietly, "What are you going to do with me?"

"I always heard that you people—arsonists—were crazy," the man said, "and now I know it. So I'm going to tell you—once—what I'm going to do with you. I'm going to get out of this valley before the fire kills both of us. And then I'm going to take you to jail and lock you in it. And I hope that's where you stay for the rest of your life."

The boy didn't even seem to be listening to him as he said, "The fire's coming down pretty fast, isn't it?"

The man looked up toward the mountains and was

suddenly overwhelmed by the enormity of this fire. The whole sky was black with smoke, with great tongues and rivers of fire flowing through it. The roar of it was like faraway thunder that never stopped.

The man looked back at the boy. "That's the first sensible thing you've said, so we're getting out of here."

"How?" the boy asked.

"On the horse, dummy."

The boy's voice was vague again, and he began shifting his feet, moving a little to the man's left. "On the horse?" he asked, and kept on moving slowly around the man, toward the horse.

"You don't think we can just walk out of this, do you, you idiot? We'll be lucky to get out on the horse. I'll get on first and then swing you up behind me."

The boy said, "The horse looks tired."

"He *is* tired," the man yelled. "And so am I—of you. So shut up."

"You want me to hold the horse while you get on?" the boy asked, moving toward the horse's head.

The horse, trembling now with fear, began coughing, the sound deep and rasping, and his eyes seemed wild and rolling with fear, his ears laid flat back.

"I can get on this horse without anybody holding him," the man said. Then he suddenly turned on the boy. "Listen, kid, all I need is for you to try to run. So if that's what you're thinking, forget it." He leaned down and pointed his finger right into the boy's face.

"If you think you can get away from me while I'm getting on the horse, try it. Because, I tell you this, I *hate* you and I'd love to have an excuse to run you down with this horse. I mean, run all *over* you."

The boy, standing beside the horse's head now, and the man, standing beside the saddle, looked at each other for a moment. Then the man said, "So don't move," as he turned and began adjusting his saddle bags to make room for the boy to ride behind him.

That done, the man turned his back to the boy and reached for the stirrup.

The horse, coughing and nervously moving, made it awkward for the man, but he finally got his foot in the stirrup and was about to pull himself up when the boy slapped the horse on the neck with his open hand.

The sound of it cracked and the horse, startled, jumped sideways, yanking the man's hand loose from the saddle pommel and pulling the stirrup away from his foot, leaving him standing there on one foot, the reins still in his hand.

The horse kept moving, coughing hoarsely as he wheeled and began to run, stumbling awkwardly as he went.

And the man stood there, both feet finally on the ground, and watched the horse disappearing into the smoky haze.

Slowly then, as though unbelieving, the man looked at the reins in his hand and followed the thin leather straps with his eyes as they sagged in a smooth arc down to the ground.

The horse's bridle was lying on the ground. Somehow the throat latch that held it on the horse's head had come unbuckled, and the bridle had slid over the horse's ears when it jumped away, and slid down his face, and fallen off, pulling the bit out of the horse's mouth.

The bright metal bit lay on the ground, still wet from the horse's tongue and with little flecks of foam drying on it.

The man slowly raised his head and watched the horse.

The horse was running better now, twisting and turning among the trees, the stirrups and leathers flapping wildly around.

As the man watched, the shape of the horse faded and then disappeared into the smoke.

The man did not want to believe that his only escape from this fire—the horse—was gone. He looked down again at the bridle lying on the ground and then up again toward where the horse had disappeared.

And then, as though the man had been slapped back into the real world—this world of awful flame and smoke and roaring—he turned and stared at the boy.

His hand moving slowly, his forefinger uncurling from his fist, the man pointed down at the bridle. His voice was shaking as he said, "Did you unbuckle that?"

The boy looked down at the bridle and then up at the man. "Yes, sir."

The man opened his other hand and threw the reins away as though they were something dirty. And then, with his hands clenched into fists, he turned to the boy. Slowly he said, "I am going to *kill* you!"

The boy backed away from the man's fury and said, in a small voice, "I wish you wouldn't, sir. I'm sorry about the horse. I just thought—"

The man yelled, interrupting him, "What you *didn't* think is that letting the horse go threatens my life."

The boy said weakly, "But the horse looked so tired and sick. Do you think he could've run anywhere carrying both of us, or even one of us? Wouldn't he have fallen down?"

The man said sternly, "That horse was the only way we could have gotten out of this fire alive."

"I'm really sorry, sir. I just thought the horse ought to have a chance."

The man, wanting to knock this kid down, said, "I want you to just *stop* thinking. Because you're crazy. Really crazy. You let the horse go, so now we're in for it. As far as I'm concerned that serves you right—to get burned alive by the fire you set. But, I don't see why I have to go with you. With my horse I could have gotten out."

"Maybe we don't even have to," the boy said.

The man stared at him. "Have to—*what?*"

"Get out," the boy said.

The man said it slowly so the boy would understand it. "Kid, get this through your crazy head. From now on you do *exactly* what I tell you. If you try another crazy trick like that I am going to—*hurt* you. You understand?"

"Yes, sir."

"Okay. Now our only chance of getting out of this fire alive is to go where the horse went. Maybe we won't get out, but I tell you this, we're going to take a swing at it. So start running."

"Yes, sir."

The man wheeled and began to run toward where the horse had disappeared.

He had run only a little way when he glanced over to check on the kid.

What he saw enraged the man, for the boy was running away in a different direction.

With fury driving him, the man caught up with him and grabbed him by his red shirt. Then he yanked him backwards with such force that the boy's feet flew out from under him and he landed hard, sitting on the ground.

The man stood over him, quivering with rage. "Didn't you hear what I just told you? You run with me. You do what I tell you to do!"

"Yes, sir," the boy said, sitting on the ground and

looking up at him. "I only wanted to get my back-pack."

"Backpack! What do you need with a backpack? This is no picnic; we're running for our *lives*, you dumb, crazy kid!"

"It's right under that tree," the boy said, getting up. "And we need it."

Before the man could grab him, the boy leaped away, ran to the tree, and picked up a small bundle. Carrying it in his arms, he brought it back and showed it to the man.

The man hated to waste any precious time with the backpack but, remembering that these arsonists are crazy, dangerous people, he knew he had to make sure that this kid didn't have some sort of weapon hidden there. A knife, perhaps, or even a gun. Or maybe some sort of bomb that could kill him.

The backpack was a crude canvas sack with some tattered ropes to carry it with. As the boy watched in silence, the man rooted around in it, pulling out some canned food, a pair of old tennis shoes, some clothes, a canteen full of water, and another canvas sack holding what felt like a skinny sleeping bag. The man squeezed this with his hands to make sure nothing solid was in it and then stuffed all the junk back in and threw it back to the kid. "Now all you do is *run*. With me!"

Around them as they ran the enormous forest fire was moving in a great semicircle, devouring everything as it roared down the slopes of the hills toward the valley they were in. The trees were exploding like cannons, their leaves and branches shooting out great gouts of flame while, on the ground, other flares and outbursts of flame were rising from the thick, burning brush.

Smoke towered up into the sky like gigantic thunderclouds, the bottoms of them glowing an ugly red from the flames, the centers dark, the tops a paling gray.

As the man ran, he pointed toward a gently rising slope of ground beyond which there was as yet no sign of smoke or flame. "That looks like the best way out," he yelled at the boy.

"Maybe," the boy said.

The man was running fast, his arms and hands fanning aside the low branches, his booted feet crashing through the brush around his legs.

As he got closer to the slope things looked better all the time, and the man was beginning to believe that they could beat the closing ring of fire; it might be just a little alley clear of flames, but even if they had to run through the fire itself it might be thin enough to let them through without killing them. Just a few burns; maybe a few serious ones, but they'd be alive. "We're going to make it!" he yelled.

There was no answer from the boy and suddenly the man felt that something was wrong—that he was alone.

He paused and looked back and what he saw outraged him.

That kid was far behind, just loping easily along, taking his own sweet time as though his life were not being threatened by anything at all.

For a moment the man thought: Let him die in these woods.

But then a sort of pride changed his mind. It was his job to get this arsonist out of here; to put him in jail. And if he did he'd get a lot of credit for it; maybe they'd even make him Senior Tower Patrol.

"*Run!*" he yelled at the kid. "You better get moving or you'll be sorry. Shuck out of that pack and get moving, understand?"

"Okay," the boy said and ran faster, catching up with the man.

Then they ran together toward the slope.

After a while, slowing down a little to catch his breath, the man said, "What's the matter with you, anyway? Don't you want to live?"

"Oh yes," the boy said, "but running takes a lot of energy. We might need it more later."

"We need it *now,*" the man yelled at him. "If we get past the foot of that slope we might be in the clear. The wind's blowing right for us. So shuck out of that backpack and let's go."

The man started running again, but after a little while glanced at the boy and saw that he was still carrying that backpack.

"Get rid of that!" the man yelled at him. "Drop it. Or I'll drop it for you, maybe taking one of your arms off with it."

"Yes, sir," the boy said, stopping under a tree, and with a slow deliberateness that infuriated the man, began untying the rope that held the pack on his back. Then, handling it as though it had some fragile glass in it, the boy carried it over and laid it down against the trunk of a tree.

"Now *run!*" the man ordered. "You're going out of these woods with me, understand?"

"Yes, sir," the boy said, his answer sounding vague and uninterested.

The man noticed then that, as they ran, the boy kept looking back at something, and then looking sharply from side to side.

Suspicious, the man asked, "What are you looking at?"

"The trees," the boy said.

"You run beside me, boy," the man said sternly. "And don't get smart. You're coming out of here with me, and I'm going to put you in jail. You can count on that."

"Yes, sir."

They ran together, stride for stride, the boy staying close to the man.

That's better, the man thought. I'm finally getting it through this crazy kid's crazy mind that he hasn't got a chance. That this is the last fire he'll ever set, the last woods he'll ever burn. Or anybody's house. In jail they won't let him even light a match for the rest of his life.

As they reached the foot of the slope and started around it, the boy went crazy again, stopping and saying, "Mister, you're taller than I am."

"So what? Run."

"Maybe you ought to look around," the kid said.

"At *what?* Run!"

"To see where we're going."

"I *know* where we're going. *Out*. So run!"

The boy was very polite. "Maybe if you went up on the slope a little way you could see better."

The man slowed his pace and looked ahead.

Now there *was* fire in front of them. He could see it flickering among the trees to his right and as he watched he saw that it was moving across their path.

The man stopped running and looked around, fear crowding back on him again. "I'm going up on the slope," he said, and then added threateningly, "And so are you."

"Fine," the boy said happily.

They had to fight their way up the slope, crashing through the thick, dry underbrush, which seemed to fight back, thorns and twisted branches grabbing and holding them while the low branches tore at their faces. What the man hated most was the time it was wasting, but, as he kept on going, he knew that he had to reach the top in order to see the way out—if there was a way.

They broke through finally and came out on a flat, almost clear area. In the middle of it was a huge boulder, half embedded in the ground, that stood up like a monument.

"I'll get up on that rock and see what's what," the man said.

"Do you want me to go with you?" the boy asked.

"You think you're really smart, don't you? Well, you're not. When I get up on this rock and you try running away, all you'll run into, kid, is fire. Lots of it. Plenty of it."

"Then I'll wait here, sir," the boy said.

"You'd better," the man warned and turned to climb the boulder.

The sides of it were so steep he had to climb on all fours, hands and knees and elbows and feet pulling him up to the top.

Still on hands and knees, the man rested a moment, panting in the smoky air, then pushed himself slowly upright and stood straight.

On top of the boulder the man turned slowly, his eyes scanning the area all the way around.

For the first time since he had been a child the man felt like crying.

-2-

The man standing on top of the boulder felt all the muscles in his legs and knees growing weak as he kept slowly turning, his eyes searching for some place in the forest where the leaves were green and there was no flickering of the red and yellow flames.

The fire was *everywhere,* in some areas close, in others far away, but it was everywhere. The whole sky was dirty with smoke, blackest above the high ridge where the fire had started; thinning here and there, but no blue showed, no sunshine could get through it. Because of this, the forest had lost its colors. The leaves were no longer green; everything was a dead gray, even the wild flowers were an ugly gray. The only colors were in the awful yellowish red flames.

The wind was *insane.* It was like a wild animal running amok, blowing a gale from the north, and then from the south, swirling without steadiness or pattern. And the wind was so hot, so dry, and so heavy with ashes that it felt solid as it struck the man from, it seemed to him, all directions.

The man had barely strength enough to get down off the boulder. At the bottom, his body just seemed to give up, all strength spent, and he collapsed into a sitting position, only the rock against his back holding him up.

The boy stood above him, looking down at him, and said quietly, "The fire's all around us, isn't it?"

The man heard him, heard the words he said, but they did not register in his mind, for the man was not thinking about the present, about *now.* He wasn't thinking clearly about anything.

"What?" the man asked.

"The fire," the boy said slowly. "It's all the way around us, isn't it?"

The man understood that and nodded, but then began to talk about something else. "Isn't it funny," he said, "how much difference only one second can make?"

The boy stood there and watched the man lift his hand and try to snap his fingers, but they only made a dull sliding noise.

"One second," the man said, staring out at nothing, "I was looking for you. On the horse. And when I saw that I might get trapped in the fire I decided to give up. I was turning the horse away, the reins were against his neck and I was pressing with my knee, and it would have taken only a second more to turn him away so that I would never have seen you running through the woods. But in that one second—just that one second—I heard you screaming. And I turned the horse back."

"We'd better go," the boy said.

The man was not listening to the boy and went on talking. "The funny part is," the man said, "that all I wanted to do was catch the arsonist and put him away where he could never set another fire like this. Never burn up anything again. Never kill anything again, not even a little squirrel."

The boy said quietly, "When the fire comes down this slope, it is going to be very hot."

But still the man ignored him, as though he weren't there. "The funny thing is that I didn't even have to catch you," the man said, still staring out at nothing. "I could have turned away and ridden out of here. I could be sitting right now in Charlie's Diner with a cup of coffee and a danish."

Then he raised his head slowly and looked up at the boy. "Because the way you were going would have taken care of everything. You were running straight into the fire, running and screaming like crazy. I didn't have to stop and arrest you. I could have let you go on running and the fire would have taken care of everything. After those flames caught you, you wouldn't kill any more animals, kid, you wouldn't have killed *anything* again. Ever."

The boy held his hand down to the man and said, "Please, let's go."

"Okay," the man said, taking the boy's hand and

letting it help pull him to his feet. Then, suddenly, the man began to laugh. He looked down at the boy and patted him on the shoulder. "Yeah," he said. "Come on, ol' good buddy, let's go. Let's go get burned up right now. No use sitting around waiting for it. Hunh? Isn't that right, kid?"

For a moment the boy stood gazing steadily at the man, and then he said quietly, "You stay here, sir, and I'll go get my backpack."

For a long time the man just stared at him, dead-eyed, but then something happened in his brain and he was suddenly back in the real world.

And he was, just as suddenly, furious. His voice shook as he yelled at the boy, "*Backpack!* You dumb jerk, what do we need with your lousy backpack? You think we've got time to get hungry? We don't need any water out of that beat-up canteen. We don't need any old tennis shoes. And we don't need a sleeping bag."

The boy's voice was slow and firm. "Yes we do."

And then the man stood over him and talked to him, his voice full of fury. "You've gotten me into all the trouble I need. From now on, kid, I don't want any more of your advice. I don't want any more of your smart remarks. I don't even want to hear you open your mouth. From now on, you don't talk. Do you understand that?"

The boy's eyes were glistening with tears of pain

but he did not cry as he stood looking directly at the man. "Am I still under arrest?" he asked.

"Yes, you are! No matter what happens to me in these woods, I'm going to accomplish one thing. You're going to be my prisoner right up to the end. Understand?"

"Yes, sir," the boy said.

The man glared at him and turned and began walking slowly up the slope. Then, as though talking to himself, he said, "What we need is a farm. With some plowed fields. Where there's nothing to burn. That's what we need. Get out in a field; dig down in the dirt if we have to."

The boy asked, "Would there be farms here? Isn't this a national park?"

The man whirled around. "Didn't you hear me? I told you to keep your big mouth *shut.*"

"Oh," the boy said.

The man turned away and began looking around, his eyes squinting because of the smoke. Then he leaned forward a little, concentrating.

Without turning around he said over his shoulder, "What's that black spot? About halfway up the slope?"

"A cave," the boy said.

For a second the man stood still, staring at the black cave mouth, and then he went crazy.

The boy watched him as he began running up toward the cave. His running was wild; furious. He ignored the thick underbrush and let it tear his clothes and rip his skin as he plowed through it.

After the man reached the cave and disappeared into it, the boy, making his way slowly, followed him, stopping at the cave mouth and peering in at where the man was already sitting down, looking at all the blood on his arms and legs and trying to pull his clothes together.

When the man glanced up and saw him, his voice was happy as he said, "Come on in, kid, the water's fine!"

The floor of the dirt cave was bone dry, the dust rising in small clouds around his knees as the boy crawled in and sat down beside the man.

The cave was small, going straight back into the hill, with only the mouth of it following the downward slant of the slope.

The man sounded almost hysterical as he cried, "Isn't this great? Man, this is pure salvation. Ha! We'll just sit out this fire, kid. Let it burn past us, and then we'll walk out of here without even a singed eyebrow. Man alive, this is *great!* Wonder how it got here?"

The boy looked around at the tool marks in the solid clay. "Looks like some miner started digging here and then gave up," the boy said.

"Yeah," the man said, his voice calmer now, "that's what it looks like." Then he leaned back against the dirt wall and took a deep, slow breath. "Man oh man, how lucky can you get?"

"Not very," the boy said.

The man turned slowly and looked at him for a long time before he said quietly, "Kid, I don't want you to talk any more. I don't want to hear any more of your crazy remarks. Okay?"

"Okay," the boy said.

The man patted his shirt pocket with his fingers and then reached in and got a pack of cigarettes that had been mashed flat by something. Then from another pocket he got a paper book of matches. Taking out a cigarette, he made it round with his fingers and tapped one end of it on his thumbnail before he lit it.

He took a long drag on the cigarette and blew the smoke slowly out of his mouth, rounding his lips as he did it.

The cigarette seemed to relax him and he slid his heels out along the cave floor.

Now the man's voice was almost gentle as he said, "You can't help it, kid. To be what you are, you have to be crazy. Sane people just do not go around setting things on fire. Fire scares *us*, you see? And we don't get a kick out of setting something on fire and watching it burn—watching it destroy things and kill things. That's the difference. You get a kick out of it because you're crazy. We don't."

"Sir," the boy said, "You've got things all–"

The man interrupted him, but his voice was still quiet. "Kid, I asked you not to talk any more. So I'll be obliged if you'll just shut up."

"There's not much use, is there?" the boy asked.

"Would you pay any attention to a crazy person?" the man asked reasonably. "Would you go into an insane asylum and listen to all those ding-a-lings telling you what to do? No. So neither do I."

He took another drag on the cigarette, blew out the smoke again, and said, "At first I hated you. You, personally. But now I don't. I just hate what you are. It's like when I was in the war. I never did really hate the people who were shooting at me. Or hate the people I was shooting at. I figured that they were there for the same reason I was. Some big shot in our government said, 'Let's have a war,' and some big shot in their government said, 'Yeah, let's have a war.' So we had to go shoot at each other.

"I didn't hate them. I hated the war. The war itself."

He dragged on the cigarette again and went on. "That's the way it is with you. I don't hate you. I hate arson. I hate having things set on fire for no reason. . . . Do you know what I do for a living, kid?"

The boy shook his head.

"I patrol the towers. You ever see those high steel towers that go all the way across the country?"

"With the high-voltage wires?"

"That's right. That's what I patrol. You'd be surprised at how much vandalism I get." The man looked at him and laughed. "One kook even tried to knock down one of our towers with a bulldozer. Now, that was a dumb thing to do because if he'd knocked it down that high voltage would have wiped him out. . . . And hunters. They're almost as crazy as you are. They can't find any animals to kill, so they stand there and shoot at our wires and insulators. Now that is really dumb. If a guy cut one of those wires with a rifle bullet and it fell on him it'd be–ZAP–instant bacon."

The man dragged on the cigarette again, then studied it as he flicked off the ashes. "That's what I do. Get on my horse and ride the fire lanes under our towers all day long or, on the night shift, all night. Looking for kooks with bulldozers, or radicals with bombs, or hunters shooting at our wires. And I watch for fires that people like you and the campers and hikers set. All day long on my horse."

"Do you see what your smoke is doing?" the boy asked.

The man ignored him. "So far, I've been lucky. But down on the sector south of mine they've had a lot of trouble. Some arsonist down there has set more than seventy fires in the last month."

The man took another drag and then looked at the boy. "I've been lucky–until now. Until you came along." Then he pointed the cigarette at the boy. "Hey! Maybe you're the arsonist who's been setting the South Sector fires."

"I am not an arsonist," the boy said quietly.

"Of course not," the man said sarcastically. "You tell me that you set a fire in the woods, but you're not an arsonist."

"Isn't an arsonist somebody who sets fires for money?" the boy asked. "A man who gets paid for setting a building on fire so somebody can collect the insurance? Or a person who sets fire to a house to burn up his enemy, or maybe his family? I didn't get paid. I didn't want to hurt anybody. So I am not an arsonist."

"That doesn't make any difference. There's a word for what you are. Pyro . . . pyro . . . something."

"–maniac," the boy said. "Pyromaniac. *Pyro* is the Greek word for 'fire' and *mania* is Greek for 'insane excitement.' I am not insane. Or even excited. I'm just scared."

The man gave a snort of laughter. "Tell me a story, kid. You're crazy as a Bessy-bug. Really nuts." Then he drew on his cigarette again.

The boy said, again, "Do you see what your smoke is doing?"

"Smoke? What do you mean?"

"Doesn't smoke usually float upwards?"

"Sure it goes up. Because it's hotter than air. So it

always goes up." the man said. "See what I mean, kid? You're crazy."

"Yours isn't," the boy said.

The man looked around, searching. "Isn't what?"

"Going up."

The man took a drag and blew the smoke out of his mouth. Then he watched it.

The smoke tried to rise, but something drew it downward.

It flowed down to the man's stretched-out legs, flowed along them, and then flowed on across the floor of the cave until it disappeared, flowing down the slope of the hill.

"Must be a current of air in here making it do that," the man said, watching the last of the smoke flow down and out of the cave.

"Maybe so. Or maybe it's the wind outside blowing down the face of this hill that's sucking it out that way."

"So what?" the man asked.

"Nothing," the boy said. "Only, one time, I think it was in Oregon, there was a forest fire, perhaps as big as this one, and some fire fighters got caught the way we are, with the fire all around them and no way to get through it. So they hid in a cave, like this, only bigger. They thought they'd be safe in there."

The man took the butt of the cigarette between his thumb and middle finger and flicked it against the wall of the cave. It made a little spark and bounced down to land near the mouth of the cave. It lay there, the smoke being sucked down and out.

"They would be safe," the man said. "Well, they'd be safe as long as there was nothing in their cave to burn. No shoring timbers or anything like that. Just dirt, like this one."

"The fire killed them," the boy said quietly. "All."

"Then there had to be something in there that burned."

"No, sir. There was nothing in there that burned. It was a rock-walled cave."

"Oh boy, there you go again," the man said, laughing. "So tell me how all those fire fighters got burned up in a rock-walled cave."

"They didn't get burned up."

"Just scared'em to death, hunh?"

"No," the boy said seriously. "When the fire came past the mouth of the cave, it was so hot and the wind was so strong that it sucked all the air out of the cave and there was nothing left for the men to breathe. So they died in there. All of them."

"What are you trying to do, scare me? Making up stories like that. We're safe as a church in here, so shut up, will you?"

"The fire's coming down the slope now," the boy said, "so we'd better get out of here."

"And go–where?" the man asked.

"To get my backpack."

The man looked at the boy with disgust. "We've already been through that backpack scene, kid. So simmer down. We're okay in here. The fire isn't going to burn us and there's going to be plenty of air to breathe. When the fire goes by we'll walk out of here like nothing happened. Believe me, that's the way it's going to be."

But the boy started crawling toward the mouth of the cave.

"Where're you going?" the man demanded.

"Out."

"*Sit down!*" the man commanded. "You're not going anywhere. Remember, you're still under arrest."

The boy, on hands and knees, looked back at the man and quietly said, "Please, sir, I want to go out."

That irritated the man. "I don't care what you want. When I tell you to sit down you–sit down."

"Sir," the boy said politely, "when the fire comes down the slope it is going to kill whoever is in this cave."

The man laughed at him. "Now I'm convinced you're crazy. Because everything you say is exactly backwards. Now here's the way it really is. When the fire comes down the slope whoever is *outside* this cave is going to get barbecued."

The boy thought about that for a while, then said, "One of us has got to be wrong, don't you think, sir?"

"No. You're wrong."

"There's a way to find out," the boy said.

"Find out what?"

"Who's wrong."

"Kid," the man said, "didn't anybody ever teach you to listen? I talk to you and you don't listen. You don't even seem to hear me. Inside this cave you're safe. Outside this cave is suicide. Now did you hear that?"

"Yes, sir," the boy said. "I heard you the first time, but I still think we don't agree." Then the boy smiled at him. "Wouldn't it be interesting to find out who's right?"

"How?"

"Well, one of us could leave the cave and go outside and the other one could stay in here. Then the one who's still alive would be the one who was right, wouldn't he?"

"There you go again," the man said. "Everything backwards. So just sit down and shut up."

The boy's voice was firmer now. "Sir, I want to go out."

"Well, you're not going to. When you're under arrest you do what I say."

"If I try to get out will you stop me?"

"You're right, I will."

The boy sat looking at the smoke from the cigarette butt flowing out of the cave. Then he looked up at the man. "If I tried to get out so hard that, to stop me, you'd have to kill me, would you do that?"

"Kill you?" the man asked.

"Yes, sir."

"Well, let's put it this way," the man said, "I don't want to kill you. I don't want to kill anybody. But you're under arrest, so if you try to escape it would be my duty to kill you if that was the only way I could stop you."

"What good would that do you?"

"It wouldn't do *me* any good," the man snapped. "It just happens to be the law."

"Then," the boy said quietly, "you'll have to do it."

Before the man understood this, the boy moved, scrambling fast out of the mouth of the cave.

Out there he fell and tumbled down the slope, but by the time the man reached the mouth of the cave the boy was on his feet and running.

The air outside was now filled with smoke, so that in a matter of seconds the boy had disappeared in the thick underbrush.

The man moved back into the cave and sat staring out at the smoke swirling around the mouth of the cave.

Who would ever know, the man asked himself, what happened to the kid? Who would know that he'd even seen the kid? Who would know that the kid was an arsonist?

Outside the cave now it was murder. From the amount of smoke and the heat he could feel, the fire must be very close. To go out there was suicidal.

No one would ever know, he decided. None of his superiors would ever find out. Nobody could blame him for not bringing in the arsonist who had set this fire.

Then, through all this clear thinking, there came doubt, and a shapeless fear.

What if, by some crazy chance, that kid was right? the man wondered. What if there really had been that fire in Oregon or wherever it was and those men in that cave had died from lack of air?

The man crawled to the mouth of the cave and looked out.

The intense heat burned him and the force of the wind sweeping past the cave mouth seemed to suck the air out of his lungs.

In a sudden wild panic the man shoved himself out of the cave only to find himself in a hurricane of flame and wind and a terrifying roaring.

When he breathed, all he got was a painful, burning, and useless intake of pure heat that seared his throat and the tissues of his lungs.

And the hot, blasting wind knocked him down and rammed him down the slope until he was stopped by the boulder.

As he fought to get up, a sad little thought drifted through his terror.

That kid was wrong. He was going to die out here.

In the cave he would have been safe.

The kid was wrong.

–3–

The man, at last on his feet again, started to fight his way back up the slope to the cave but soon gave up, for the wind was too hot and dry and strong, and the flames too close.

And so he stood helplessly and looked with great longing up at the safety of the cave that was now denied to him.

A furious blackness of smoke boiled up, torn and swirled by the wind, and below it there was a waterfall, an avalanche, of pure fire flowing down the slope and over the mouth of the cave. Some perversity of the wind seemed to catch the fire there and turn it into a whirlpool, a maelstrom, of flame.

Even if he could reach the cave, the man knew that he could not get through that wall of fire covering the mouth of it. And, as he watched, he wondered whether anything inside the cave could live for long. Perhaps there would be air left in it, but it would be so hot it would burn a man's lungs out.

Then the man had no more time for small thoughts,

for the fire was all around him, racing through the woods to reach him, and all he could think about now was running for his life.

Torn, burned, bleeding, and battered, the man came down the last of the sloping ground and ran on across the floor of the small valley. Here, without the hills and canyons forming obstacles that compressed and heated the already searing wind and forced it into even greater velocity and pressure, the air was a little calmer, a little less threatening, and the flames were not moving as fast.

After the turmoil of the cave and down the slope, this level place seemed comparatively tranquil. There was wind, but it was steady, and there was smoke, but only a thick haze of it—not that boiling blackness, lit as though by lightning with the streaks and flashes of flame.

The man, exhausted and hurt, slowed to an awkward jogging as he went on in the same mindless direction. He knew, without admitting it to himself, that this jogging along under the great, silent trees was useless. There was nowhere to go to avoid the fire closing in all around him. He would do no more to save his life by jogging than he would if he just stood still and waited for what was coming.

And at last he did stop, too defeated to go on, but still not admitting it. Instead, he told himself that he was only going to rest a moment: restore his strength, catch his breath, and then he would get up and fight again, battling against the fire.

He slumped down under one of the trees and rested his back against it. Knowing what he would see if he looked out at the fire, and not wanting to see that any more, he let his head fall forward so that his eyes could study a flow of blood coming from a tear in his leg where a thorn had ripped him. The blood looked very thick and dark in the smoke-darkened air, and it ran sluggishly down his leg, stopping when it reached the torn cloth of his trousers.

"Have you got a match?"

The sound and the words were so alien that the man thought that they must be some trick of his memory. How many times, he wondered, still watching the flow of blood, had smokers asked him for a match? A hundred? A thousand? And how many times had he asked other smokers for a match? A lot of times.

Peculiar things happen to people when they are panicked by fire, the man remembered. One time, he recalled, a man whose house was burning to the ground broke through the police lines keeping people clear of it. The man, fighting his way past the police and then the firemen who were spraying water on the house without any hope of saving it, reached the inferno of his house and ran straight through the flames and into it.

The people standing around thought that the man must have taken this enormous and probably suicidal risk for some great treasure he had inside the house and, in a way, they admired his courage.

And then, miraculously, the man had come out again, staggering, his clothes on fire, his face and hands burned raw.

The treasure?

The man brought out only the morning newspaper, it, too, on fire.

Peculiar things. . . . There had been no voice speaking to him, the man decided. There *couldn't* be any voice here.

"Mister, I need a match!"

The man raised his head slowly, seeing first the legs, the blue denim trousers. And then on up to the blazing red shirt and finally to the face of the boy.

The man had always thought that if people were crazy, that craziness would show in their eyes. You could just look at insane people and know that they were insane.

Ever since he had caught this boy, those calm gray-blue eyes with their steady, direct way of looking at you had disturbed the man. He had kept searching for the craziness in the eyes he knew existed in the boy's mind, but he had never seen it.

And it was not in those eyes now as the boy looked down at him.

"A match?" the man asked vaguely, and automatically, without having to think about it, patting the pockets of his shirt where he always carried his cigarettes and matches.

"Yes," the boy said.

The man sat there on the ground, staring up at the boy.

After all the running they had done, all the fighting their way through the vicious underbrush, the boy looked so *neat*. His clothes were not ripped and torn as his were, the thorns had, somehow, not touched him, for the man could see no blood anywhere on the boy.

Perhaps it was this almost irritating neatness that made everything suddenly become real to the man.

He sat there and began to laugh. "Man oh man," he said, "that's the craziest thing you've said so far."

Then the man pushed himself to his feet and stood close over the boy, his body threatening him as he glared down at him. "So you want—a match. With the worst fire I've ever seen burning all the way around us, you want—a match."

Then the man swung his arm in an angry, wild gesture. "Isn't what you've already done enough for you?"

"If I had a match," the boy said quietly, "we could set a backfire. Then we could stay downwind from it and let it burn out around us. Then, when the main fire reached here, there would be nothing for it to burn, so it wouldn't be so hot. I'm afraid that if we don't, and just stay here, we aren't going to have enough protection."

"Use your own matches," the man said with barely controlled anger. "You've got plenty of 'em. All ready to set some more fires if this one doesn't kill enough things to suit you."

"I haven't got *any,*" the boy said. "I never had . . . I mean, I only had one match. And I used that one."

Again the man automatically patted his shirt pocket and now recognized that it was empty. "Well, now, ain't that just too bad? Because I haven't got any either."

The man stood there a moment looking without hope for some avenue, some small alley, of escape: even some place where the fire looked thin enough to race through with a chance of living.

There was now only the complete ring of solid fire around him, which didn't even offer him a choice of direction. It would meet, and stop, him wherever he went.

And then that kid started yakking again.

"Maybe setting a backfire wasn't such a good idea anyway. If the wind changed before it had burned far enough away from us, it wouldn't have done any good. It wouldn't have done *us* any good, either."

The man, ignoring the kid, wandered listlessly, his lungs hurting, his body hurting, his mind dead.

The boy, walking along beside him, said, "So what do you think about getting in the creek?"

The man heard the words but, for a few more steps, they didn't mean anything. Then, suddenly, they did. He whirled on the boy. "*Creek?*"

"Creek," the boy said. "A brook, a stream, a little river."

Almost yelling, the man said, "*Where,* kid? Which way?"

"I'll show you," the boy said, beginning to trot through the woods. "It'll help us for a while anyway. Be cooler."

"*Run!*" the man ordered, racing past the boy.

As they ran along together, the boy seeming to guide himself by various trees and rocks, he said, "It isn't very deep, or even wide."

"How do you know it's even there?"

"I waded across it this morning."

The man, staring ahead through the thick, dark haze, could see no sign of any running water: only the forest, silent now as though waiting for the death coming toward it from all directions.

Was this just some crazy idea? the man wondered, fear again overriding the hope he had had. Was the kid's twisted mind just making this up so he'd feel better?

Then the kid stopped running and caught the man by the arm. "You wait here," the boy said. "Right under this tree."

"Wait a minute!" the man said. "What's going on? How come I wait? Where's the creek, kid?"

"Not far. So if you stay here I won't have any trouble finding you."

The man stared down at him. "What kind of game is this?" he demanded. "Where're you going?"

"To get my backpack," the boy said. "It won't take long, so you wait."

"Oh no," the man said. "You're not going to get away with that. I'm going with you."

"You don't have to," the boy said. "The creek's straight ahead, so if you want to, you can go by yourself. But I have to come back here to get my bearings again."

The man stood in silence looking down at the boy as he tried to make his mind work clearly; to make it put aside for a moment the great, defeating fear clouding it.

If there really is a creek, the man thought, that's salvation. If there isn't, if this is some trick the kid is pulling, then—what difference did it make? Where he would be in these woods when the fire reached him would not be important.

"Straight ahead?" the man asked.

"Right past that twisted oak and then just keep going."

"Okay," the man said, "but I want you to know that I don't buy your story about getting your backpack.

So if there's no creek you're going to be in *big* trouble."

The boy looked up at him and laughed. "You can say that again." Then he ran off into the smoke.

– 4 –

It seemed to the man that he had been running for hours through this dark, smoky forest where each tree looked like all the others, although each was different. The twisted oak the boy had talked about didn't exist, and as the man ran on, his lungs now stabbing him with pain at every breath, exhaustion making every step feel like the last one he could take, he gave up the last hope he'd had. His weary running, really only a blind staggering through the woods, had become mechanical and senseless. There was no use running, and yet he ran.

His mind had grown confused. There were no longer any clear thoughts forming and being worked out. Instead there were only dim scenes of meaningless things, small visions and memories.

Suddenly one of these became very clear.

It had been a long time ago, in another place, a different forest fire, and he had been walking through the woods after the fire had burned through them and the ashes had cooled and lay like a thick, gray carpet covering the earth.

The thing that had hurt him then more even than the sight of the murdered, limbless trees was the dead animals lying in the ashes. There were charred skeletons of all manner of things—large and small—lying there in the ashes. And all of those skeletons, he had noticed, were contorted, twisted out of shape, as though each one of them had died in great agony.

Would he, the man wondered now, look like that when some stranger came walking through this forest after the fire had passed and the ground had grown cool? Would his bones show the pain of his dying?

And, he wondered, would the boy's? A smaller heap of bones, but saying the same thing?

The man wandered on, and as he went he couldn't determine whether the underbrush seemed thicker and more resistant to his passage now only because he was at the point of total exhaustion or whether it was in fact thicker. And, oddly, seemed not as dry and brittle as before. The leaves seemed greener and softer, the limbs more pliable, bending against the weight of his body rather than resisting and then breaking off.

Now something was really wrong. His feet had grown monstrously heavy and the trousers around his ankles seemed weighted with lead.

He could go no farther.

He let his head drop, his bleary eyes staring at the ground.

Something was *wrong*. There was no earth there; only a smooth, gray layer with, he could see dimly, rounded rocks and pebbles that seemed to him to waver slowly and aimlessly.

The man, his back aching, leaned slowly down and touched the gray surface.

It was water!

Straightening, he stumbled out into the middle of the small stream and then collapsed into the water until he could feel the cool, wet water with his lips. It took all his strength to keep from going on under it.

The coolness of the water, the wetness, were the most delicious things he had ever felt, and they seemed to let his strength flow slowly back and to let his mind clear of the fog of terror that had clouded it.

At last, he was safe!

It was a long time before he even thought about the boy, but when he finally did, he spun around to look back in the direction he had come.

He could see only a few yards through the pall of smoke drifting with the wind.

Raising his face clear of the water and cupping his mouth, the man began yelling. He wished he knew the boy's name as he sat in the creek yelling again and again, "Hey, kid! Hey, kid!"

There was no answer, no movement except the wind-twisted smoke and the crowns of the trees resisting, the pine needles and oak leaves already drying from the heat, shriveling up and dropping off, to drift with the smoky wind.

It was useless to yell. His voice couldn't carry against the constant, dull, increasing roar of the fire.

And it was useless to go look for the boy. He could be anywhere out there, still searching uselessly for that tattered bundle of junk.

In the water with the man now, other things began to appear. All manner of bugs and flying insects came floating down the slow-moving stream, some of them riding twigs and fallen leaves as though these were rafts aboard which they could escape.

And small animals came swimming down the stream. Wood rats, and field mice, squirrels and woodchucks and moles, some of them making small squeaking noises as they floated past him, ignoring him.

Fish swam by, bumping against him as though blind with fear, and turtles, some swimming with their heads out of the water, others like dark submarines hurrying down the stream.

To all these things the man was nothing. He was no longer something to be feared, something to either avoid or bite or sting or claw. He was only an obstacle in the path of their escape. Nothing hurt him even though many of the creatures bumped against him and were moved around him by the current.

Suddenly there was a sound he had not heard before coming down through the tumult of the fire. A dry, slow, flapping sound which, as it grew louder, changed to an almost lisping noise, like *shop shop shop.*

Helicopters!

The man looked up, trying to force his vision to penetrate the solid darkness of the air above him, but he could see nothing.

And the fire fighters in the choppers couldn't see him either, and the sound died away.

As the man lowered his head he thought that he saw something move in the forest, but when he looked again, thinking that it had been a deer, he saw nothing.

But then, again, something moved and now he fixed his eyes on it.

The boy!

There he was wandering around in the woods.

That crazy kid. With the fire coming closer all the time, there he was wandering around with that stupid backpack cradled in his arms. There was no purpose in his movements, no reason for what he was doing. Just wandering around in the smoke.

"Hey, kid!" the man yelled, standing up in the water and waving his arms. "Over here!"

The boy turned to look at him and called, "Hi."

"The *creek!*" the man yelled. "Come on. Get in."

"Yes, sir," the boy said, but he kept on wandering.

The man watched with amazement while the boy strolled around, looking up occasionally at the trees above him, then down at the ground, or stopping to touch a bush, or examine the dry grass at his feet.

At last the man realized that the boy was now truly crazy. Completely crazy.

As the man came wading out of the creek it was apparent to him that the awful threat of the fire had finally unhinged the kid's mind.

The man came up beside the boy as he stood idly examining a small area of ground, and his voice was gentle as he said, "Come on, kid, the water's fine." And his hand was gentle as he took the boy by the arm.

The boy pulled away but did not run. Instead he stooped and with great care put the backpack down on the ground. Then he straightened and stood looking around. "That's as good a place as any," he said.

"Yeah, kid," the man said gently, "that's a good place. So come on now and feel how good the water is. Real cool and wet. You'll like it."

Walking together back to the creek, the boy said, "I'm glad you found it. I was afraid you'd get lost."

"I didn't get lost."

The boy stopped at the bank of the creek and put his hand down in the water. "Still cool," he said, smiling up at the man.

"It's just great!" the man said. "Wait'll you sit down in it. Best feeling I ever had."

They waded out into the water, the boy sitting down in it before the man, who was taller, did.

"Feels good," the boy said. "I was getting hot out there."

"You know it," the man said, blowing his breath out across the water. "Lot of critters in the water with us, but they don't pay any attention."

"I guess they're as scared as we are," the boy said.

The man knew now that he was right. This kid, being an arsonist, was a little crazy to begin with, and now fear had made him totally crazy. "Are you scared?" he asked gently.

The boy looked downstream at the man and smiled. "I'm too afraid to be scared."

The man didn't understand that. "What does that mean?"

"I don't know."

The man laughed. "I don't either. Tell me, kid, how did you find that backpack of yours in all this smoke and fire?"

The boy seemed surprised by this. "It was where I left it," he said in a perfectly reasonable tone.

"Of course it was," the man said. "I shouldn't have asked such a dumb question."

"Did you hear the choppers?"

"Yeah."

"Do you think they're fighting this fire now?"

The man raised his head and looked around at the ring of fire. "They're fighting it all right, but that isn't going to do us any good. They can't stop what's coming for us before it gets here."

The boy slowly stood up and looked around, then waded a little closer to the bank and peered through the bushes at his backpack.

"What are you looking for?" the man asked.

"Just looking."

"At your backpack?"

The boy nodded and sat down in the water again.

The man said, "You know what bothers me, kid? There's nothing in that pack except junk, but you don't mind risking your life to keep that thing. So you go hunting around, with this fire coming down on us, to find it and bring it here. Then what do you do? Instead of bringing it here to the creek you leave it lying out there in the woods where you know darn well it's going to get burned up when the fire reaches it. Tell me, kid, *why?*"

The boy seemed to think a long time about that simple question, but at last said, "Because I don't know what the water would do to the tents. It might ruin them."

The man's mind couldn't handle this. "What difference does it make? You don't need any tents. You won't need them for a long time. Long enough for them to dry out if they get soaked. Isn't that better than letting them burn up in the fire?"

"That's the trouble," the boy said, frowning. "They weren't made for this environment, so I just don't know."

The man shook his head slowly, his chin brushing

back and forth across the water. There was no use talking to this boy. No use at all.

Then the boy surprised him. Still frowning, he said, "I wish I'd asked my father what would happen to them if they got wet."

The man laughed at him. "Your father would've said the same thing I did."

"Maybe he would have," the boy agreed. "Because he would've known."

"What's your old man know that I don't know?"

"Oh, I didn't mean that," the boy said. "Only, he's a pyrologist."

"A what?"

The boy's voice was vague as though he was thinking about other things as he said, "He studies heat."

"He makes a living studying heat?" the man asked.

"Not exactly that," the boy said, as he stared around at the water and the trees. "It's the chemical decomposition of things caused by heat that he studies. What happens to things when they get hot."

The man sucked some water into his mouth and then squirted it slowly out, making a little ridge across the surface. "That's kind of sad."

"He likes doing it," the boy said. "He knows more about heat than almost anybody."

"No," the man said quietly, "what I mean is that your father spends his time fooling around with fire and his son turns out to be a pyromaniac, a firebug, an arsonist . . . that's what's sad. Does he know what you are, kid?"

"No," the boy said. "Because I'm not."

The man smiled at him tolerantly. "It's a funny thing, but you can talk to everybody in a jail and every one of them will swear that he's not guilty of what he's in there for. Not one."

"That's an interesting reaction," the boy said.

"When they put you in jail, you'll say the same thing."

"I just did," the boy said.

"Yeah," the man said, "you're not guilty of anything, are you? You just set a forest fire that's going to do millions of dollars' worth of damage, that's going to kill every living thing in the woods, that's going to cost thousands of dollars to put out, and hundreds of years for these trees to grow back. That's nothing, is it? Not guilty."

The boy didn't seem to be listening to him as he sat there in the water, staring out at nothing. "I must've run pretty fast to get down to where you caught me," he said, not looking at the man.

The man laughed at him. "I can't blame you for wanting to change the subject. Yeah, you must have run like that great stripy bird, boy, because when that fire took off, it *moved*. There was a wind blowing across our tower road at around fifteen, twenty miles an hour, and when it hit the fire you set it must have moved it down the mountain at forty, maybe fifty miles an hour. That's moving!"

The man looked over at the boy. "But you know when a person panics he can do miraculous things. I read about a boy who was working under his car when it fell off the jack and pinned him. That kid's mother–and she was just a little bitty woman–saw it and came out there and lifted up the whole back end of that car so he could get out. With her bare hands. People can do things like that when they panic." The man suddenly laughed. "Maybe you grew some wings and flew down those hills."

"I only ran," the boy said quietly. "You saw me, didn't you? Wasn't I wearing this same red shirt?"

"Same shirt, kid, so don't try to alibi your way out of this."

"I'm not. I'm just wondering how you got down here so fast."

"In the first place, I was on a horse, and instead of having to run through the woods the way you did, I came down one of the fire lanes where it was wide open."

The boy said slowly, "I wonder why I didn't try to get out of the way of the fire instead of just running in front of it."

"Like I said, when you panic you do crazy things. When that fire started, I mean to tell you, boy, it was an awful sight to see. Just all of a sudden it was huge and moving very fast. If I'd been in front of it the way you were, I'd've panicked too, because it was terrifying. It's a miracle you're still alive, kid. The way that fire took off I would have sworn that nobody could outrun it. Sixty, maybe seventy miles an hour? No *way*."

The boy sat in silence for a long time, then looked over at the man. "You must have really wanted to catch me to risk your life that way."

"Well, that's sort of like panic, too. When you get angry, I mean really *mad*, you don't think about risking your life and things like that. I wanted to catch you, boy, because I *hate* people who set the woods on fire."

The boy's voice was sad as he asked, "Would you hate me as much if you knew that I didn't do it on purpose? That setting the fire was an accident?"

The man thought about that for a moment. "Well, maybe not as much. But you've got to hate anybody who's stupid enough to set the woods on fire—accident or no accident."

The boy asked quietly, "If you were sure I wasn't an arsonist, that it really had been an accident, what would you do to me?"

"Kid, it isn't up to me to decide what happened. If somebody sets the woods on fire and I catch 'em, all I do is take 'em to the police. It's their job to find out how it happened, not mine."

"Oh," the boy said, "so no matter who it is, or what

happened, you take them to the police. Don't you even tell the police what you think happened?"

"Man oh man! You really twist things around, kid. Of course I tell the cops what I think happened."

"Suppose somebody set the woods on fire accidentally, and you knew it was an accident, and he was a good friend of yours–maybe he'd even saved your life–would you take him to the police?"

The man studied the boy for a moment and then grinned. "I see what you're getting at, kid, and it isn't going to work. Don't get me wrong, because, personally, I like you. You're a nice, polite kid; maybe you're real intelligent; I don't know. But you can't convince me that this fire was an accident. And–" The man stopped and laughed a little. "You haven't saved my life. In fact, you've been trying to kill me ever since I caught you."

The boy was surprised and hurt. "Kill you? Me?"

"Okay. You let the horse go. Wasn't that trying to kill me?"

The boy's voice was close to crying. "Sir, I was only trying not to let the horse get killed."

"Sure. It's okay for me and you to get killed but not the horse. And what about in the cave? All that yakking about no air. I thought then, 'Oh oh, this kid's trying to kill me again. . . .'" The man's voice slowed to a stop and he sat in silence idly watching all the animals and bugs and fish going down the creek. At last he raised his head and looked over at the boy.

"There's something about you I don't understand. Did you really think we'd get killed in that cave?"

The boy said quietly, "We're not in it, and we're not dead."

"That's right," the man said, "and this is what I don't understand. If you had really wanted to kill me you could have."

"I never have," the boy said.

"But you *could* have killed me. You could've sneaked over to this creek without ever telling me, because I didn't even know the creek was here. But you did tell me." The man stopped talking for a long time, and then said, "That's sort of like saving my life, isn't it?"

The boy looked steadily at him with those calm, grave eyes. "Not necessarily, sir."

-5-

A deer came running down the creek, its huge brown, soft eyes filled with terror as its hooves skidded on the slippery stones of the creek bed, so that its movement did not have that flowing grace of a deer running on the land.

The man and the boy watched it coming, and as it got close to the man they could see that it did not even recognize him as an enemy, but carefully stepped over him and went on, its white tail flicking with fear as it disappeared into the smoke.

And then a raccoon came swimming strongly down, three of her little children riding on her back, holding tight to her hair, the black and white bands across their faces making them look as though they were laughing—like kids on a merry-go-round. Their chattering was a thin, squeaky sound, like the voices of children.

A fox swam along beside an opossum, and rats and squirrels and rabbits; birds, beetles, bugs, lizards, and worms came down the creek. Fish and eels and turtles flocked together under the water, all headed down the stream.

The creek with its teeming life was one world, the forest being devoured by fire was another. Over both of them was the incessant sound of the fire. There was the constant roaring and whining of the wind, and this sound was filled with the sounds of explosions as air pockets in trees went off like cannon, and rocks, heated beyond their endurance, cracked open with the sharp noise of rifles. And small things: beetles and larvae in hard shells snapped like gentle popcorn in the awful heat of the fire. And the burning trees made their own sounds as the fire clawed at their trunks and raced through their leafy crowns, crackling and burning and killing.

And above the worlds of creek and forest there was the smoke and flame of the fire which killed even the light of day. The darkness around the man and the boy was not the darkness of night, nor the darkness of a cloudy day. It was the darkness of *black air,* for the air itself was so thick with ashes that the sunlight could barely penetrate it.

Upstream the fire was now crossing the creek in many places, overcoming with its heat even the soft green underbrush that grew in a band on each side of the creek, the roots nourished by more water than those of the underbrush of the forest.

Awed and frightened by this holocaust, the man and the boy had not spoken for a long time, but now, suddenly, the boy began talking.

"Rattlesnakes are funny," the boy said, as though chatting in a schoolyard. "Did you know that rattlesnakes are deaf?"

The man looked closely at the boy, wondering whether the sight of the great fire around them had tipped his mind again. "I didn't know that," he said.

"They are. Deaf."

"Let's don't talk about snakes."

"Don't you like snakes?" the boy asked.

"Not much."

The boy *was* crazy, for now he laughed. "I heard a man say one time that there were only four kinds of snakes he didn't like. Big ones, and little ones, and live ones, and dead ones."

The man's smile had no humor in it, and he said, "That's about the way I feel, kid."

"But rattlesnakes are funny," the boy said again. "When most land snakes get in the water they swim like water snakes, but they seldom bite you. Maybe because they don't want to open their mouths. But rattlesnakes in the water will bite you. Because they don't like to swim. And they don't like getting wet, so they coil up tight and float high up on top of the water. That way they're ready to strike, and they're irritated too."

"Kid," the man said, "I asked you to shut up about snakes. So just stop talking about them. Okay?"

"We might need to," the boy said. "Rattlesnakes are very interesting. They're not only deaf, they can't see very far either, so they depend on catching their food by smelling and feeling with their noses and their tongues. They're very sensitive."

"I am not listening to you," the man said, gazing out at the ugly colors of the flames moving through the smoke.

"Perhaps you'd better listen," the boy said quietly, "because there is a big rattlesnake floating toward us now and if we don't do things right he'll bite us—and we'll die."

The man jerked his head around to look upstream.

The body of the rattlesnake floating on top of the water, moved only by the current, was as big around as the man's arm and was tightly coiled, the string of rattles sticking straight up from the center of it and vibrating so fast it made a grayish brown blur.

The triangular head of the snake was up, the neck curved so that the big, flattish head was parallel to the water and waving slowly back and forth as though searching for an enemy. The forked tongue kept darting in and out of the little triangle of its lip as though it, too, were searching.

The sound of the rattles was very dry and, to the man, terrifying.

The boy said quietly, "The main thing is not to move at all. Don't jerk your head around again, or even move it to watch him. Don't move anything at all because that's what attracts their attention and we don't need that."

The man was now too afraid to move and only his eyes swiveled to watch the snake. In a moment an eddy of the current carried the snake out of his angle of vision.

"I can't see him any more," the man cried, his voice shaking.

"You don't need to, because I can."

"What's he doing?"

"Rattling," the boy said calmly. "The rattles are made out of keratin, the same stuff that makes horns and fingernails, even hair and feathers. Depending on the temperature, they rattle at about forty-eight cycles per second."

"Stop yakking!" the man said angrily. "What's he *doing?*"

"Just floating down the stream," the boy said. "People are too big for rattlesnakes to eat, so they don't bite us unless we bother them."

"Where is he?" the man asked, his voice breaking.

The boy's voice was now a little stern, but quiet. "You're trembling. That's shaking the water. He can feel that and it'll scare him. What you need to do now to stop shaking is to take some deep, slow breaths.

Real slow. Real gentle. And think about something else. What would you like to think about? Have you got a wife? How about your horse?"

Terror was shaking the man's whole body, but he forced himself to breathe slowly and his fear subsided a little and his voice grew calmer. "Is he getting close to me?"

"Closer," the boy said. "I had a Shetland pony one time and when he got the bit in his teeth he'd *take off*. The only way I could stop him was to get my feet up under his front legs and spread them apart until we fell down. Kind of rough, but it was the only way I could stop him. He was very stubborn."

The man sounded excited now. "I'm going to get under the water! He can't reach me down there."

"That might not be a good idea," the boy told him. "You might have to come up for air at the wrong time. Maybe under him, or close enough for him to hit you."

"Okay," the man said firmly, "I'm going to kill him!"

"You haven't got anything to kill him with."

"What can I *do*?"

The boy's words were slow now. "Stay still. Don't move. Don't move anything, even your eyes. Keep looking right at me. Don't talk."

"Is he coming closer?"

"Yes. So please stop talking."

This angered the man. "Why don't *you* shut up?"

The boy said quietly, "He's floated past me. And he

can't hear me or feel the heat of my breath. But he's very close to you and can feel the heat of yours. So don't talk. Don't move. Don't blink."

The man sat, now petrified by fear, his eyes fixed on the boy's face as he wished the boy would tell him that the snake was gone.

Instead, the boy said, "Mister–get–ready. The snake is going to touch you. When you feel the touch of his body you must not jerk away or move at all. His body will feel cool, and hard. Like a car tire, but gentle. He won't bite you unless you make him do it."

The man waited . . . and waited. . . .

The boy's voice was very soft. "Mister–*now!* Breathe slow and smooth. Don't move. Look at me."

The sound of the rattles seemed to be all around the man, pressing down on him with that hard, dry threatening vibration.

And then the snake's coiled body collided gently with the man's head just behind his left ear.

The boy watched the slow current roll the snake's body slowly over the man's ear and then onto his face, rolling slowly like some sort of inflated rubber toy.

"You're doing great!" the boy whispered. "Just keep breathing slowly and don't move."

The snake, as it was moved by the sluggish current, kept its head pointing directly at the man's head, the long, forked tongue slithering out through the little triangle, the tips of it flicking at the man's skin or hair.

And then the movement of the snake's body, still touching the man's face, stopped, held there by some eddy of the current.

The boy watched as the snake drew its flat head back, the muscles rippling as though gathering strength to drive the fangs into the man's skull.

The boy whispered softly, "You're doing fine! But I've got to move him on down the stream. So—now—don't move *anything*. And—now—stop breathing. Hold your breath for as long as you can."

Then the boy cupped his hands under the water and pushed them gently toward the man's head, pushing a body of water against him: water that moved smoothly and gently and did not alarm the snake as it dislodged him from the man's face. The snake floated away from contact with the man and was caught in the current again and floated on down the stream, the sound of the rattling dying away.

"He's gone!" the boy said. "And you did really good! You did fine!"

The man's eyes stared at him blankly and his breath came quivering out of his throat and then he collapsed face down in the creek, his whole body shaking violently.

The boy moved quickly down beside him and lifted his head out of the water.

"It's all over," he said to the man as he held his head in his hands. "Relax. That snake rolled right around your head and you didn't move a muscle. He was watching you, too, and was ready to strike if you had moved. But—you didn't."

The man lay in the water, exhausted. "Funny feeling," he said weakly. "Cool and sort of smooth. Yeah, like a tire."

"I don't think I could have stayed as still as you did," the boy said. "Just watching him drawing back made me shake all over."

"I was too scared to shake," the man said. Then he looked at the boy. "At first all that yakking you did aggravated me, kid. But when you kept on, it began to work, I guess. Sort of took my mind off what was happening. A little, anyway, because I couldn't help listening to you and that helped a lot. But I tell you this, I never thought about my wife or even my horse. I—" The man suddenly stopped and stared at the boy. "Hey . . ." he said. "I could have watched that snake coming. I could've seen him all the time. But you didn't let me, did you?"

"Well . . ." the boy said vaguely.

"Naw!" the man said, grinning at the boy. "You didn't let me. You told me not to turn my head, you told me to keep on looking at you, because if I didn't it would shake that snake. . . ." The man began to laugh. "But you knew all the time that it wasn't the snake that was going to shake, it was *me!* Man oh man, if I'd watched that thing floating toward my head I'd've—come *apart*. That snake could've been so old he didn't have any teeth and he'd have still scared me to death. So that's what you did! . . . Man, that was the longest week I ever spent."

The man and the boy sat side by side in the water and laughed together.

–6–

Their laughing didn't last long because the great fire coming toward them was so awesome that laughter couldn't live there.

After a while the man said, "Kid, I wish I understood you."

The boy said softly, "I wish people would stop saying that."

But the man didn't hear him and went on, "That snake . . . This is the first time since you let the horse go that I've really thought that we had a chance of getting out of this fire alive. You and I. But if we do I'm going to have to report you to the police. It's my duty to do that, kid."

"I know," the boy said.

"The thing is," the man said, "I think *you've* believed for a long time that we were going to get out; maybe right from the first. So that's what I don't understand."

"What?" the boy asked.

"That snake. I'd never been in the water with a rattlesnake. I didn't know what to do. If you'd left me alone I'd've goofed and that snake would have bitten me. I don't think anybody could survive being bitten in the face or the head by a rattlesnake as big as that. The poison would get into your brain too fast, don't you think?"

"Yes, I do."

"All right, then," the man said, "you knew you had a good chance of getting out alive and you knew that if I got out with you it would mean big trouble for you. But if that snake had killed me it wouldn't have been your fault and you could have gone away without anybody knowing that you started this fire. So why did you go to all that trouble?"

The boy turned slowly and stared at the man. "Because I was afraid the snake would damage you."

The man slowly shook his head from side to side. "After all the grief I've given you today, you didn't want anything to 'damage' me?"

"Grief?" the boy said.

"You know, knocking you down. I really didn't mean to hit you so hard. And arguing with you; the cave and everything. And the horse. Kid, that's what I don't understand."

The boy's eyes had changed and become softer and warmer and his voice was slow and unsure. "Mister, please don't say that again."

"Say what, kid?"

"About understanding. A lot of people say they

don't understand me, and there's nothing I can do about it. I wish I could. I know a boy that everybody likes because, I guess, everybody understands him."

The man looked at the boy's face for a long time and then said, "Oh." Then he smiled and pushed some water gently at the boy and said, "That's not the way it is, kid. People like other people without having to know exactly how they think or what they're going to do. I bet a lot of people who don't understand you like you just the same." The man laughed and pushed some more water. "*I* sure don't know what you're going to do or say next and *I* like you. That's why I'm so sorry I have to do my duty."

The boy looked at the man for a moment longer and then turned his head away and sat in silence.

After a while the man started talking again. "I haven't heard any more planes or choppers. But I guess it's their main job to protect towns and people's houses. Out here there's nothing to burn except trees."

"And us," the boy said.

"Not us!" the man said, and laughed. "But what do you think we ought to do when the fire hits us? Try to stay under the water long enough for it to go on by? That might take a long time. So maybe we'd better lie on our backs with just our nose and mouth out of the water. And keep our shirts over our faces, and keep them wet all the time?"

"Maybe," the boy said, but didn't seem to be really interested in the problem.

The man wiped his face with his hands and looked around. "This creek's got more critters in it than it has water," he said, as he looked at the almost solid mass of living things pouring down from the hills. "But the sad part is how many critters never made it to this creek and are dead now. They'll be lying in the cold ashes tomorrow, their bones all twisted up from the pain they had when the fire took them."

The boy said slowly, "Don't you think that perhaps some things could stay alive on the ground? Somehow find some way to protect themselves?"

"No way, kid. This isn't an ordinary forest fire like those set by lightning when the woods are a little wet from the rains and the fire just burns out the underbrush without hurting the trees. Actually, that kind of fire is good for the forest because it cleans out the bushes that are taking a lot of water and food from the trees. But this thing is what they call a fire *storm.* A fire that kills *everything.*"

The boy's voice sounded vague, as though his mind was on something else. "Everything?"

The man waved his arms toward where the fire glowed like a towering wall of flowing light. "What could live through that?"

"Hasn't it slowed down a little?"

"It always moves faster up and down the hills," the man told him. "Because of the wind. Down in the valleys like this the wind isn't as strong, so the fire moves slower, but it still *moves,* making its own wind."

"Slow enough for somebody running really fast to stay ahead of it?" the boy asked.

"Whoa," the man said. "Hold the phone, buddy. There's no use thinking that we can get out of this water and make a run for it. This creek's the safest place in the world."

"I wasn't thinking about *us* running."

The man settled back in the water. "Fine. Because we're just going to sit right here and watch this fire go by."

The boy turned and looked directly at the man. "When you first noticed the fire, did you try to put it out? In the beginning it wasn't much of a fire, was it?"

"As a matter of fact I did try to put it out, but I got to hand it to you, kid, when you set a fire it's a *mover*."

The boy asked quietly, "Is that when you saw me running? When you were trying to put it out?"

The man nodded.

"Why didn't you try to catch me then? Wouldn't it have been easy to do with the horse?"

"Kid," the man said, "let's be friends as long as we can. Let's don't aggravate each other. On Tower Patrol we don't fool around. When there's a fire the first thing we do is try to put it out, not go chasing after the guy who set it. And if I can't put it out I get on the walkie-talkie and call it in to our fire units. After I get through all that is when I start chasing you arsonists."

"Couldn't I have gone a long way by then?"

"Yeah. But so could that fire. And–" Suddenly the man stopped talking and sat in the water frowning. Finally he looked over at the boy. "Something's been bothering me ever since the first time I saw you, kid. So how about giving me a straight answer? Something I can understand."

The boy didn't say anything and the man went on talking.

"You and I have been trapped by this fire for a long time," he said slowly, as though thinking up the words as he went along. "And up until now I thought you were nutty as a fruitcake. But there's one thing you haven't done since I first saw you down here."

"What?" the boy asked.

"To begin with," the man said, "when I first saw you, you weren't running *away* from the fire, you were running right into it. Now, you've got to admit that that's really *crazy*. And you were screaming. You haven't screamed since."

"Screaming?"

"See? You were so crazy you don't even remember it, but you were screaming like a maniac. At first I thought you were yelling somebody's name. A girl's name–Annie. But now I know you were just screaming because you were crazy. And running in the wrong direction."

The boy didn't look at him as he said, "Annie?"

"Whoa!" the man said. "Wait a minute." Then he leaned forward and studied the boy's face. "Maybe that wasn't just screaming. Maybe you really were yelling to somebody." Then the man settled back in the water, thinking, and as he thought he flicked his fingernail against his front teeth. And after a while he said, "Up until now I've been too busy with this fire to do much thinking, but now I'm beginning to put this thing together. I'm beginning to add things up. And subtract a little, too. . . . Now–from the time I saw this fire start, and tried to put it out, and radioed it in, couldn't have taken more than a few minutes. And then, man oh man, me and that horse came down the fire lane fast. A lot faster than any man or any kid running on his feet could have come down through all those trees and bushes. So–what happened?"

"What happened?"

"When I got down into this valley you–were–already–*here*. Running around screaming like crazy. What does that add up to, kid?"

The boy looked straight at him. "That I'm ready for the cracker factory."

"Maybe you are, but that's not what it adds up to. Do you know what I think? That you were in these woods with somebody else. That you weren't just screaming. You were calling somebody's name. Annie."

"Annie?"

"That's what it sounded like." Then, talking slowly as he thought it out, he said, "How could you have gotten down here before I did on my horse? Even with the time I spent trying to put out the fire and call in and all. . . ." the man stopped and stared at the boy. "You *couldn't* have gotten down here before I did. It's at least five miles as the crow flies from where the fire started to where I found you, and really rough country all the way. *Nobody* could have gotten down here that fast." The man stopped and then his voice was gentler. "Kid, have you been lying to me?"

"Lying?"

"Well, maybe not lying. But maybe—kidding me?"

Then the man sat in the water, flicking his teeth with his fingernail. "I'm beginning to figure this out. You were in the woods with somebody else. Some girl with a name like Annie. Only she was up on the ridge near the towers and you were down here with that cockeyed bug net."

The man began to nod his head judiciously. "Five *long* miles. You weren't anywhere near the ridge, so you've been kidding me all along." He pointed his finger at the boy and smiled. "Son, you didn't start this fire."

The boy said, "I did."

"Come on, kid, who are you trying to protect? Some gal you're in love with?"

"I did it by myself."

The man grinned at him. "By yourself? Then why did you tell me a while ago that you had some *tents* in that backpack? Not *a* tent—*tents*. If you were here by yourself, why would you need more than one tent?"

"I might meet somebody who needed a tent."

The man smiled and then studied the boy for a long time and when he spoke again his voice was very gentle. "Annie set that fire, didn't she? Probably just fooling around with matches. An accident. But she set it and then got caught in it. The only way your Annie could have escaped was to run toward the towers. She didn't do that, kid, she ran the wrong way. I saw her, dressed just the way you are, and with a bug net too. . . . So, kid, it doesn't make any difference now. Nobody can do anything to her now. Nobody can put her in jail. So there's no use kidding me any more. No use trying to protect anybody, because Annie is somewhere up in those hills with all the other dead things—the trees, the animals, everything. I'm sorry, but what difference can it make now?"

The boy's gray-blue eyes were no longer calm as they stared at the man with stony rage. "You—stupid— . . . ." the boy said. "It makes all the difference in the world! . . . There's nobody named Annie. That was my brother up on the ridge and his name is Danny. And my father was proud of . . ." The boy stopped abruptly and blinked his eyes, then said quietly, "My father is proud of Danny. He liked him a lot. So here's what you don't understand, mister. If Danny is dead I am not going to let you make my father ashamed of him. I'm not going to let you or anybody say that Danny started this fire on purpose, or by accident, or any other way. I'm not going to let you call Danny all those names you called me—arsonist, firebug, pyromaniac—because if my father thinks that Danny had anything to do with starting this fire it will hurt him; it will make him ashamed." The boy stopped and looked at the man for a long time. Then he said quietly, "The only thing that doesn't make any difference is what you say about me. If you don't tell the police that I started this fire I'll tell them that you're lying."

They sat in silence, just looking at each other, until the man said quietly, "I really am stupid. And I'm sorry."

"I am, too," the boy said, "for what I called you. I got a little mad."

"I was stupid," the man said, "because there's a better way to do this. A lot better. Because there's no use blaming a dead person, is there? So let's do it this way. I'll say that I didn't see *anybody* on the ridge. I didn't see *anything*. Just, all of a sudden, a fire burning in the woods. That way nobody but you and I will ever know what Danny did. I give you my word that I'll never say anything else. Okay?"

Those eyes looked steadily at the man for a moment and then the boy said quietly, "Okay. But I still don't think that Danny had anything to do with this fire. My father trained us too well for Danny to make a mistake like that."

"That's right, son," the man said gently. "We don't know anything about how this fire got started. All we know is that Danny got caught in it."

– 7 –

The man and the boy had been sitting in the creek for some time. They hadn't talked any more because the approaching fire was so enormous and so threatening that any talk seemed trivial. And their throats were sore from breathing the smoky air.

Almost like the twinkle of stars they could see burning bits of wood and leaves floating in the darkness above them. But the color was not the crystal clearness of stars, it was the dull red glow of fire. These burning bits fell all around them, adding to all the other sounds of the fire a thousand little hisses as they struck the water.

The man and the boy both watched a thin piece of wood, the limb of a tree perhaps, which the wind was carrying straight toward them. It glowed with fire along its whole length and little trails of fire were torn away from it by the wind.

It did not reach them, but fell to the ground near where the boy's backpack lay on the brown grass.

The man moved, and said, "I'll go put that out before it burns your backpack."

"I'd rather you didn't," the boy said.

"It's setting the grass on fire!"

"That's what I've been waiting for," the boy said.

The man tried to laugh but it made him cough. When he could, he said, "Well, here we go again—same crazy kid. But it's bye-bye backpack."

"Maybe that's good," the boy said.

They sat in silence watching this small, separate fire burning through the grass and bushes. Without the force of the great fire behind it, this one moved slowly along, burning out a circular area in the dry brush but being stopped by the greener, wetter growth along the bank of the creek.

When this fire reached the backpack it did a thorough job. The canvas sack went up in a small, quick flash, but the tennis shoes burned slowly, with gouts of black thick smoke swirling up from each one.

And then the cans of food exploded, one by one.

When the fire passed on, there was only a little heap of charred junk lying on the bare floor of the forest.

The man looked over at the boy, and slowly, the boy turned his head to look at him.

"That was Danny's gear too?" the man asked. "And his tent?"

The boy nodded.

After a while the man said, "In a huge fire like this

it doesn't take very long. It moves so fast and is so hot. . . ." His voice trailed off as he saw the tears welling up in the boy's eyes.

"You thought a lot of your brother, didn't you?" the man asked.

"I still do."

"I know. How old was he?"

"Twelve."

"And you?"

"I'm fourteen."

"I never had a brother," the man said. "I had a sister who was older than I was. Man, she beat up on me like crazy until I was about six years old. But one day I grabbed her by the hair and whopped her head up against the wall and she didn't beat up on me any more after that."

The boy looked at him and smiled.

"You ever beat up on your brother?" the man asked.

"It wasn't necessary."

"Sounds like he was a good kid. You two always dress the same way?"

"I wish you wouldn't keep on saying '*was*,'" the boy told him. "He *is* dressed the same way. My father gave us these shirts so somebody with a gun wouldn't think we were something to shoot at."

"I'm hoping the same thing you are," the man said. "That 'was' just slipped out. . . . You know, I don't even know your name."

"Murdock."

"What's your first name?"

"That is my first name. Murdock L. Turner, the Third."

"That's a good name."

The man looked at the fire for a while and then said, "If we get out of this, I'd like to see you some time . . . and your brother. I could get a horse, I mean, horses, and we could ride patrol together."

"We would like that," the boy said, and then his eyes began to glisten with tears again.

The man thought up something different to say. "Hey. Some of these fish are dead."

"I know," the boy said and reached out to a small trout floating belly up in the stream. He picked it gently out of the water and held it in both hands.

"Wonder what's killing them?" the man asked.

"The water."

"The water?"

"They've been boiled," the boy said. "Alive." Then he put the dead fish back into the water, right side up. As it floated away, it revolved slowly until its white belly showed again.

They both turned and looked upstream but could see only the dull, pulsing glow of the fire through the thick smoke.

"I guess it crossed the creek up there and got the water pretty hot," the man said.

"The water is pretty hot here."

The man, as though unaware that he was sitting in

the water, raised his hands and patted the surface. "You think so?"

"I know so," the boy said. "And it's getting shallower all the time."

"How can it get shallower?" the man asked, fear beginning to move in him again.

"The fire's boiling it away," the boy said. "Like a kettle on the stove. And when the fire gets here it can take all the water out in a few minutes."

The man's voice sounded dull. "Look, everything coming down the creek is—dead. They aren't swimming any more."

The boy didn't answer as he stood up in the water and looked out toward the fire coming at them through the woods.

"And the water's all gray with ashes and stuff," the man said. "And it *is* getting shallower. I'm going to dig down deeper."

The boy only nodded as he kept studying the fire.

It was a monstrous thing to see. The fire was coming toward them now on three levels. At the top it was burning furiously across the crowns of the trees, the wind there seeming stronger and so moving it faster. Below the crown fire the lower limbs and branches and leaves of the trees burning made a separate but equally furious layer of flame. Finally there was the ground fire, lashing its way through the underbrush and scouring the ground clean of everything that grew—or moved—there.

The air was now thick with ash and embers, and blowing, burning leaves, and the wind blew strong and hot against the boy as he stood watching.

The man, lying face down in the now shallow water, dug frantically with his hands, but the creek bed was thick with rocks and gravel and his hands made no headway, the sharp edges of the stones only tearing at his fingers.

Defeated, the man stopped digging and just lay a moment panting. And when he looked up the boy was gone.

In sudden lonely panic the man jumped to his feet, the hot, fiery wind hitting him in the face, and looked around in the smoke for some sight of the boy.

And there he was walking around in the small clear area that the burning limb had created: a small, almost circular place where all the grass and underbrush had already been burned away.

As the boy walked his feet created little puffs of ash that were caught by the wind and blown away.

"Hey, kid! Murdock!" the man yelled. "Come back! There's still some water."

The boy stopped moving, but instead of turning back toward the creek he knelt down in the ashes.

"Get up, kid!" the man yelled at him. "You haven't got a chance out there. Come back!"

When the boy continued to ignore him, the man started toward him but stopped suddenly and stared through the smoke.

There on the ground beside him, the boy had somehow formed two shapes which, as the man peered through the smoky air, looked to him like two grayish, almost silver tubes. But not smooth. They had small, rounded waves in them. Just like the body of caterpillars, the man thought.

Just like two monstrous caterpillars. Six feet long, maybe, and a couple of feet wide. Weird, horrible-looking things out there on the ground.

And the kid fooling around with them.

This insanity of the kid's seemed to be contagious, for the man could feel his own mind growing confused and indecisive. What to do? Go grab the kid and drag him back to the creek?

Was there time enough for such a struggle?

Or leave him there, fooling around with his horrid worms, until the fire came close enough to drive him back to the creek?

What to do?

Still undecided, the man walked slowly back to the creek and down the bank and out to the middle of it.

There was no water.

-8-

Where the fine, clear, cool water had been flowing a little while ago there was now only a damp mass of gray ashes, lumpy with the dead bodies of all manner of things. Animals, the hair burned away and the skin raw and bloodstained; fish, boiled and swollen and broken open; turtles burned alive in their shells, the skeleton feet and heads and tails drooping from the openings.

The man, standing there looking down at this filthy, horrible stuff, felt cheated. He didn't think that, after all he had done to escape from this fire, he deserved to be treated this way. It wasn't fair for the creek to dry up and abandon him, leaving him nothing more to protect himself from the fire storming toward him.

It just wasn't fair.

Something strong and warm, but gentle, took his hand and pulled at it, and he looked down and saw the boy.

"Come on," the boy said, "it's time."

"Time?" the man asked, his mind vacant.

"Just come," the boy said, pulling at his hand.

Stumbling along, being pulled by the boy, the man followed him through the woods toward the grayish silver caterpillars lined up facing each other on the burned-over ground.

They stopped at the tents and the boy said, "You get in that one."

"No," the man said, "I don't want to."

"Just get in," the boy said. "Go in feet first so your head will be this way."

The man stood there, stubbornly shaking his head.

"It's the only thing we can do," the boy said. "So get in."

The man yanked his hand away. "No! What's the use?" He turned to glare at the fire swirling toward him. "I'm going to make this fire catch me. I'm not going to give up and be caught lying in some tent."

"Running around won't do any good," the boy said. "The tent might."

"Might what?"

"Do some good. So, please, get in. I'm going to get in mine."

The man stooped down and looked into the darkness of one of the tents. "What's in there?"

"Nothing."

"So why should I get in it?"

"So I'll know where you are," the boy said.

The man straightened and looked at the fire again.

"Oh," he said, "what difference does it make?"

"Perhaps a lot. So let's get in."

"Okay. You sure there's nothing in there? No snakes or anything?"

"There's nothing."

"Ugliest tents I ever saw," the man said, then began to back into one of the tents.

"Be careful not to knock down the supports that hold it up," the boy cautioned him.

Now the man could see that the only thing keeping the tent in place was some thin hoops of some kind of dull metal, or plastic.

When he was all the way in, he lay on his stomach and then, resting his chin in his hands, looked out into the smoky air.

The boy was still out there fooling around in the ashes. He had taken off the red shirt and was trying to tear it.

The man said, "We aren't going to look very pretty when this is over."

"Maybe not," the boy said, at last ripping the shirt in two. Then he hunted around until he found the battered canteen. "Still got water," he said, as he unscrewed the cap.

Wadding up the two pieces of shirt, the boy carefully poured the water on them as the man in the tent lay watching. The boy seemed very concerned that he pour out the water in equal amounts on each piece of the shirt, and that interested the man. This kid was going to keep on doing crazy things right up until the fire took him, the man thought, his mind so stunned that only remnants of thoughts like that drifted through it.

The boy came over and handed him one of the pieces of wet shirt. "When the fire comes, hold this over your nose and mouth and then put your face right down on the ground to breathe where there'll be more air."

"Oh, sure," the man said, taking the cloth.

At last the boy crawled into his tent and lay like the man, his chin in his hands, his still, calm eyes looking across the narrow space between him and the man.

Then the boy smiled at him. "In a little while we'll find out," he said.

"Find out what?"

"Maybe something, maybe nothing. I don't know."

"Whatever," the man said dully. "We'll know we're dead. But at least, kid, we gave it a good try."

"I think we did," the boy said seriously. "When the fire hits don't forget the shirt."

"Kid," the man said, "I'll never forget this shirt. If I hadn't seen it I'd still be up there under the towers, safe as a church."

"It's almost here," the boy said. "It's a good thing this area got burned over first so when it comes there won't be anything on the ground for it to burn. There'll just be a lot of fire and smoke."

"That's just great," the man said. Then he strained his head around to look back into the tent. "I just don't like being in this caterpillar. It's ugly."

"Caterpillar?"

"That's what it looks like to me. A big, ugly, dead caterpillar."

"It does, doesn't it?"

The man lay in the ugly thing for a moment longer as he looked across at the boy, then he began to move. "I don't like it in here," he said. "If I'm going to die I want to do it standing up. I want to see what hits me. I want to fight. A little anyway. Not just lie here like I'm already dead."

"You're not going anywhere," the boy said sternly. "You stay there."

"No way, kid," the man said.

But before he could move the fire reached him.

9

The fire struck the two small tubes of silvery cloth with an awesome force. The flame and wind beat down on the fragile hoops holding the cloth up with such weight that they almost collapsed above the man and the boy.

The flame was so intense that the trees and bushes around them did not burn the way logs burn in a fireplace. These things would stand, battered by the fiery wind, thrashing but still alive, until the fire reached them and, in a matter of seconds, destroyed them. Grasses, the small brush, and even young trees simply vanished into the flame and only the giant trees stood after it passed, but they were no longer trees, for every leaf and twig and branch and limb had been consumed and they stood there like great black, dead sticks.

The man could not stand it lying helpless there inside the now writhing, squirming cloth, the inside of the tube lit by a pulsing, hideous yellowish red light. The searing hot air around him was intolerable and the wet cloth over his mouth seemed dry now and every breath he took was clogged with smoke.

Choking as he yelled, he screamed at the boy, "I'm burning up in this thing. I'm getting out!"

As the man squirmed toward the entrance he saw the boy's head move outside his shelter.

The instant the boy's head came beyond the protection of the cloth his hair caught on fire, giving him a strange, unworldly appearance.

"Stay where you are!" the voice of the boy came out of the swirling fire that was his head. "You are *not* burning. You're just hot."

"Your hair's on fire," the man screamed at him.

The boy beat at his flaming hair with the wad of shirt and kept yelling at the man, "You're only hot. You are not burning." Then, as he backed away into his shelter, the boy said, "And you're not going to get any hotter."

Then the boy, still patting his smoking head with the cloth, began to laugh.

The man, staying under his tent, stared through the smoke and flame at that kid, his hair burned almost completely away, his scalp beginning now to bleed, lying there in the other shelter—*laughing*.

Even through the man's own pain and fear the sight of the boy laughing made him sad—as though he had lost a good friend.

Then the boy raised his head a little and looked across at the man. "It works!" he yelled triumphantly.

Then he rolled over on his back and began to laugh again. "It works! It works!" he kept yelling, looking up at the silvery stuff billowing around in the fire storm.

Almost as suddenly as the fire had struck them it moved on, on to other places still unburned in the forest. And as it moved away it seemed to leave a deep silence behind it.

The sad silence of death, for everything around them—trees, bushes, bugs, animals, reptiles, birds—*everything*—was dead except the man and the boy.

To the man it was like waking up from an awful nightmare and he moved as though still in the dream. Moving slowly, he inched his way out from under the cloth and stood in hot ashes, a hot but dying wind blowing against him.

The boy came out and stood beside him, the blood dry now on his head, and he seemed to the man to find it as hard to believe that they were alive as he did.

But then the boy reached down and touched the now brittle and charred cloth, the silver of it burned almost totally away, and then he said quietly, "My father is a great man."

"I guess so," the man said.

"Do you remember when those three astronauts got burned alive in their spaceship?" the boy asked.

That event was so far removed from these ashes, these dead things, this smoke, that the man had a hard time remembering it, but at last nodded.

"My father didn't think that was right," the boy said. "And so he began working on some sort of cloth astronauts could wear, or that you could make a shelter with for fire fighters that wouldn't burn. That would protect them. And," the boy said, pointing to the two tubes on the ground, "that's it. It's a special asbestos cloth my father made that fire can't burn, and the silvery stuff reflects the heat away from it so it can't even get hot enough to hurt you. My father has been working on it for a long time."

"He did good," the man said, his mind still dull. But then he asked, "Why didn't you tell me about this a long time ago?"

"I wanted to," the boy said, "but I couldn't."

"Why not?"

"Because my father wasn't sure it would work. He only tried it out in the laboratory. Never with live people in it. Danny and I told him that we'd get in the tents and see what happened, but he wouldn't let us. He told us not to use the tents except in an emergency. So—I couldn't tell you, because I didn't know."

"Well, now you can tell your old man what happens."

"He'll be pleased," the boy said. "Let's take them down so we can show him what they look like after a fire hits them."

"Yeah," the man said.

The tubes collapsed like accordions and the boy

folded them until they were very small. "You carry yours," he said, giving it to the man.

The man took the little bundle and then looked slowly around. "It's going to be a while before we can get out."

"So let's sit in the creek."

"There's no water."

"There will be soon," the boy said.

And the water was already beginning to flow again as they walked down through the ashes on the bank and out into it.

"Do you want me to put some water on your head?" the man asked. "It might make it feel better."

"Let's wait until the water's cleaner."

They sat down in the water together and splashed it on their bodies.

"It's hard to believe, isn't it?" the man asked.

"It's wonderful," the boy said. "Magic. So many things work fine in my father's lab where everything is under control but then don't work anywhere else. He gets discouraged sometimes."

The man looked at the boy and felt like crying. "That other caterpillar was Danny's, wasn't it?"

The boy could only nod as tears began to fill his eyes.

"I don't know," the man said slowly. "Maybe I could have done things differently. Maybe I could have found Danny and gotten him out under the towers where he'd be safe. I don't know."

The boy didn't raise his head as he asked, "Isn't there any way he could have escaped? Some place he could hide from the fire?"

The man thought about it for a long time. "*We* tried everything," he said at last. "We ran, we got into the cave, we thought we were safe in the creek. But the only things that saved us were your father's tents. Danny didn't have any of those things."

The boy turned away, but the man knew that he was crying now.

And he wanted to cry too, for he knew that from here all the way up the mountains and through the canyons, all the way up to the towers, everything else was dead.

— 10 —

"Murdock?"

The voice seemed to have come from among the lacy skeletons of the bushes that had burned out along the creek bank, and the boy in the water jerked his head up, staring through his tears.

The voice came again. "Is that you, Murdock?"

The boy leaped up and ran splashing through the water. "Danny!" he yelled. "*Danny!* Of coursc it's mc. Danny!"

A young boy appeared on the bank of the creek. His red shirt was in tatters and seemed to be caked with mud and ashes. His face was also caked, so that his eyes seemed to shine out of it.

"Doesn't look like you," the young boy said.

"Danny, Danny, Danny," Murdock cried, taking his brother in his arms, and they stood hugging each other and laughing.

"You look like a old bald-headed man," Danny said. "What happened to all your hair?"

"You don't look so good yourself. Come on in the creek and wash off."

As the boys waded out into the creek, Murdock said, "This is my brother, Danny. Danny, this is . . . Sir, I don't even know your name."

"Buck," the man said, standing up and reaching out for Danny's hand. "Man oh man, am I ever glad to see you! Are you hurt, Danny?"

Danny shook his head. "Just crawled on," he said. "I never been so crawled on in my life."

This puzzled the man, but Murdock seemed to understand it perfectly.

"Wash your face and you'll look better," Murdock told Danny as they sat down in the water together. "Where did you come from? Where've you been?"

Danny splashed water on his face and said, "Murdock, I have really *been.*" He lifted one foot out of the water and they could see only the top part of a sock still on it. "That is a *hot* foot because one of my shoes came off somewhere."

Murdock looked at his foot. "Kind of raw."

"Like your head," Danny told him. "You been standing on it?"

"Very funny," Murdock said. "Now come on, Danny, where'd you come from?"

"It's a long story. You got anything to eat?"

"It all blew up. So talk."

"Murdock," Danny said, "I saw a swallowtail butterfly up on the ridge that you wouldn't believe. He was *beautiful.* And *smart.* I was chasing him around with the butterfly net because he was a real specimen. And all of a sudden here was all this fire. Coming at me from everywhere. I said, 'Oh oh,' and lit out. I wanted to get out on that bare ground under the towers but the fire wouldn't let me, so I just took off through the woods."

"Downhill?" Murdock asked.

"Yeah, and I was *rambling.* I was covering ground. But every time I looked back that fire was like a dog snapping at me. That fire didn't know when to quit. You should've seen it."

"I did," Murdock said. "So?"

"So I started looking for something better than running around in the bushes because that fire was getting serious. It wasn't leaving me any room at all and it was so smoky that I ran *kerblam* into something so solid it knocked me flat."

"A rock?" Murdock asked.

"No. It was an old falling-down shack in the woods."

"I remember that old shack," Murdock said. "Didn't you know that couldn't protect you?"

"Of course I knew it!" Danny said indignantly. "But there's a well behind that shack. Did you ever see a *square* well?"

"Square?"

"The opening in the ground was square." Danny looked at his brother and smiled. "So I jumped in."

Murdock stared at him. "You just jumped down into a well? How'd you know there was any water in it? You could've broken all your legs."

"Better'n getting them burned off," Danny told him. "But I didn't just jump in. It was too dark down there to see any water, so I dropped the butterfly net down the well. It took a *long* time to fall but then it splashed so I knew there was water down there. So I got in the well."

"You're brave," Murdock said. "How'd you figure you were going to get out?"

"Who had time to figure?" Danny demanded. "That fire was right on *top* of me so I couldn't waste time *thinking*. Even while I was waiting for the butterfly net to hit, that fire burned down the shack and part of my shirt. But the well had a little roof over it and a chain on an old rusty pulley, so I grabbed both sides of the chain and went down it. Murdock, I went down that chain just like a monkey."

"I can imagine," Murdock said.

"Yeah! And down in the well there was a beat-up old bucket on one end of the chain. And a *lot* of other things. It was so dark down there I couldn't tell what they were, but they were swimming around and crawling all over me. And more and more things came jumping down. I know there was a 'coon down there because he kept talking all the time, and I think there were squirrels and snakes and lizards. All of us just swimming around with the fire roaring and growling around at the top. But you know what bothered me the most?"

"The snakes?"

"The snakes were real friendly. It was those sticky-footed frogs." Danny looked over at the man. "Have you seen them, sir? Kind of greenish and their feet are *real* sticky. They stick to *anything*. So they stuck to me, all over my head and face. They were a real aggravation, so I said, 'All you fellows have got to get off of me,' and I scraped them off and put the butterfly net over my head. Then we all just paddled around while all these burning things dropped down on top of us. I kept splashing water so none of us would get burned."

"Man oh man," the man said, "you two kids are *something* else!"

Danny smiled at him. "Murdock's the one who thinks all the time. I don't do much of that. Anyway, the fire went on by and it got kind of quiet down in the well, so I got both ends of the chain and climbed up out of there. It was sad up on the ground."

"Here, too," Murdock said quietly. "Everywhere."

"Yeah. Gray. And everything dead. I would've found you sooner," Danny went on, "but there was this sapling the fire had killed and it had fallen over, so I dragged it to the well and stuck it down in there so at least the things that could climb could get out. I think most of them could. And then, after I got started, my foot would get hot and I'd have to wait a lot for the ground to cool off."

"How *did* you find us?" the man asked.

Danny looked at him, surprised. "Sir, I knew my brother was down here in the valley catching butterflies, and I knew this creek was here, so I knew he'd be in the creek when the fire came."

"We weren't," Murdock said.

Danny turned slowly and looked at him. "You weren't in the creek?" he asked quietly.

"At first," Murdock said. "Then all the water boiled out and it dried up."

Danny looked slowly around as though trying to find some place of refuge, but when he saw none he turned back to Murdock. "Then why aren't you dead?"

Murdock smiled at him and beckoned with his finger.

The brothers stood up together and waded over to the bank, where Murdock picked up one of the folded tents and handed it to Danny.

Danny examined it, turning it slowly around in his hands, then he looked up at Murdock, his face suddenly beaming. "It worked?"

Murdock smiled and nodded.

"And you were in it?"

Murdock nodded again.

"And the fire hit you?"

"Hard."

"And all it did was burn your hair off?"

The man said, "It wouldn't have done that if I hadn't been such a fool."

Danny sat back down in the water, turning the little bundle over and over in his hands. Finally he looked at Murdock and said, "Now he'll know."

"Who—what?" the man asked.

"My father always wanted to know if his cloth would really keep you from being burned alive, but there was no way for him to find out. Now he'll know. He'll be glad."

"They were great!" Murdock said. "It got a little hot inside them. And maybe Dad can put in stronger hoops, because they flopped around a lot in the wind. But they *worked.*"

Danny looked at his brother and said, "It must have taken a lot of guts to get in there and just—wait."

"Didn't take any," Murdock said. "There was nothing else for us to do."

The man said, "Maybe it didn't take any for you, Murdock. But it took more than I've got; a lot more. I've never been that scared in my life." Then the man laughed and automatically patted his shirt pocket where he kept the cigarettes. He took the package out and opened the flap with his fingers. "They're *dry.*" Then he patted his other pocket but found no matches. As he stood up he laughed and said to Danny, "Right in the middle of the biggest fire storm in the *world* your brother asked me for a match. I thought he was crazy."

"Sometimes I think so, too," Danny said. "But he never is."

The man waded out of the creek and began rooting around in the ashes looking for a burning ember to light his cigarette with.

Murdock put his arm around Danny's shoulders and gave him a short, brotherly hug. "Good to see you. I've got to admit that when the fire was really bad I wondered how you were going to make it. I said, 'I wondered how,' I didn't say I thought you wouldn't."

"*I* did," Danny said. "I didn't have any fireproof tent. And I still say it had to take guts to get into one. Dad's ideas are always good, but sometimes he goofs in the translation."

"Not this time. He's going to be really happy."

Danny sat watching the man still looking for a light for his cigarette. "Where'd that man come from?"

"Oh," Murdock said vaguely, "he was just around." Then he looked straight at his brother. "Danny, the man and I have made an agreement."

"About what?"

"The fire," Murdock said quietly. "We know that it wasn't started on purpose. That it was an accident."

"Yeah, it was," Danny said.

"So we aren't going to tell anybody about anything. We aren't going to blame anybody. The man and I are going to say that we don't know anything about it. It was just a fire."

"It sure was!"

"Danny," Murdock said seriously, "I'm not going to ask you what you did and I don't want you to tell me. Okay?"

"If that's what you agreed to, then it's okay with me."

"Good," Murdock said and hugged him again, then took his arm away.

The man came back smoking the cigarette and sat down beside them. "I hate these things," the man said, looking at the cigarette, "but they sure calm your nerves."

"They'll kill you, too," Danny said. "My father's a pyrologist and he says that if you want to kill yourself it's better to do it with a gun or something rather than put all that hot smoke down in your lungs. You won't suffer as long, he says."

"I know it, I know it," the man said. "But I'm hooked."

Murdock suddenly stood up in the water and peered out through the smoke. "I saw something move out there. Something big, like a deer maybe."

"You couldn't have," the man said. "There couldn't be anything alive out there."

Murdock slowly sat down again but kept searching with his eyes, as he asked the man, "Do you think your horse liked you?"

"Liked me?" the man said, then laughed. "Well, he never bit me, or kicked me, but he'd throw me off every now and then."

"Did you like him?" Murdock asked.

The man looked at him for a moment and then said quietly, "Yeah, I liked him. I liked him a lot. He and I went a lot of miles. . . . Yeah, I did like him."

"Then maybe he liked you, too," Murdock said. "Maybe he's looking for you."

"No way," the man said. "Don't get me wrong, I like horses, but horses are really *dumb*. And no horse would have courage enough to come wandering back into a mess like this. Horses are scared of everything."

"Not even to look for you?" Murdock asked.

"I told you," the man said, "Horses are dumb. And *scared.*"

"People think that," Murdock said, "but maybe horses don't."

Danny turned to look at the man. "I saw a man riding a horse," he said, looking down from the man to the water.

"Where?" Murdock asked.

Before Danny answered he picked a small twig out of the water and held it between his thumb and middle finger. "When I was up on the ridge a man came by riding a horse and he was smoking and he flicked the cigarette away just like this. . . ." Danny flicked the twig out into the stream.

As Murdock and the man stared at him in silence,

Danny said, "I guess the man thought it was going to land on that bare ground they keep around those towers, but the wind caught it and blew it over into the woods. And then . . ." Suddenly Danny stopped and stared at Murdock. "Oh, golly, Murdock. I just forgot. I mean I . . ." His voice trailed off as he looked guiltily at his brother.

And then a silence fell on the three people like a weight.

And there was silence all through the forest. No song of birds, no businesslike chirping of bugs or calling of frogs. The gentle wind blew silently, for there were no leaves or pine needles to sing in it. There was only silence.

The man's face was shattered as he stared out at the murdered trees. Slowly he took the cigarette out of his mouth and pushed it down into the water.

His voice was a whisper in the silence as he said, "I did. I did do that. . . . Oh, Murdock, look what I did."

And there was silence again, but it was broken by the neighing of the horse who came wandering toward them through the desolation.